The Subtleties of Seduction

The Subtleties
of Seduction

A Novella

David Orsini

Quaternity™

THE SUBTLETIES OF SEDUCTION

Quaternity™ Books
Copyright © 2013 by David Orsini
Third Edition Quaternity™ Books 2020
ISBN: 978-1-943691-02-9
Cover Design by James Buchanan

Other Books by David Orsini

The Weaver of Plots

Schemes, Disguises, & Traps

Vanishing by Degrees

The Ghost Lovers

The Woman Who Loved Too Well

Bitterness / Seven Stories

THE SUBTLETIES OF SEDUCTION

1

The morning after her father and Malcolm Turner had arranged things so that there would be no scandal, Linda Maguire awoke feeling uneasy. She had every right to believe that she had been betrayed. She had allowed herself, perhaps as a way of easing her sister Tracy's grief over the recent death of their mother, to be caught up in a most awkward situation. The entire incident had been tinted with the moral ambiguities that she abhorred and that, she'd believed, her parents had influenced their daughters to abhor.

Casting its shadow upon them all, the episode had occurred within an extended July visit to the home of her fiancé Steven's parents, Daniel and Olivia Bradford. She, her father, and her sister had been enjoying an agreeable month of summery activities radiating from the Bradfords' superb estate in Newport, Rhode Island, while her father's own splendid home a mile away on Ocean Drive was being revised by a team of architects, landscapers and interior designers. Within the four weeks of their visit in midsummer 1920, Daniel and Olivia had provided them with every resource of their hospitality that might allay the sorrow that had not left them even six months after her mother's death.

During what was for them an essential season of adjustment, she and her sister joined a small sailing party that included her always admirable Steven. In addition, there was Ryan Turner.

Although he appeared to be a Harvard friend of the Bradfords' younger son, Aaron, he made himself far more available to almost every other young person within convenient miles of the Bradfords' imposing seaside property.

Ryan was a descendant of eminent Turners who had amassed their first fortunes in shipbuilding centuries earlier. Later they had amassed a profusion of more immense fortunes in iron, oil, and steel while acquiring the status of the legendary because of heroic exploits not only in various wars, but also in law and government. With careless assurance, he had drawn her sixteen-year-old sister into an ambiguous episode that might have compromised her. That this same Ryan Turner belonged to a family that had, through so many momentous ordeals and the most grievous personal tragedies, always maintained its obligations to the highest ethical standard, only made his wild youth's indiscretions that much more dismaying. Although he was an assertive young man nearly twenty and well-trained surely in the code of behavior that men of his class were expected to represent dutifully and instantaneously (he was, after all, Malcolm Turner's son), he did not always do his part. Too often, his actions were, if not wrong in their intention, certainly ambivalent in their resolution. By so behaving, he cast a cloud upon those friends whom he persuaded to join him in his adventures.

Yet there was something altogether appealing about the imaginative ways in which he tested himself and tested others, as well. Linda found herself still liking him because of his restless and creative approach to the world. Besides, although he had initiated the wayward trajectory of those hours, he was not the only person responsible for everything that went wrong that afternoon.

During one of the Bradfords' magnificent Sundays, Ryan casually suggested that they—Steven with her in his new, rugged yawl, and Ryan alone in his sailboat—should race against each other in winds far more vigorous than those which allowed them their recent victory in a regatta. The day was warm, with pearl-gray clouds scattering toward the horizon. The wind made the air occasionally aggressive, its heat more sullen, more palpably moist and no longer comforting.

After the day's casual rhythms betrayed their expectations, Steven's and hers, she remembered that Ryan had persuaded them to leave imperceptibly the Bradfords' grand summer party. By so persuading, he had led them to a path that compromised her sister's reputation. Unpredictable and mysterious Ryan was—with swagger so carelessly self-reliant that you believed at once the hard-bodied lankiness possessing it would treat both happiness and hardship with equal indifference. Clever and intriguing as well, he had captivated Steven and her in this first summer of their feeling they belonged to one another, though they were not yet married. He had captivated them completely, her usually reserved yet always creditable Steven and her as well, through the sheer splendor of seeing him, a vigorous youth of their class, react with such easy and spontaneous freedom to possibility's ambivalent turnings. Though several years younger than Steven and without his brutal experience of the war, he was in many ways just as knowing, just as canny about the world's bruising, addictive textures.

Subtly and plausibly he had drawn them away from the bountiful array of banquet tables with sun-gold canopies. There, in the midst of a wide expanse of greenery, visiting ambassadors and moguls, poets and scientists, and artists and philosophers mingled with crisp assurance, glad to share their hosts' ornate repast and their own animated convictions. He had led them to an enshadowed grove of lilac trees—white, lavender and crimson.

When they had arrived at the entrance to the grove, she noticed the glowing red border of berberis and verbena and amaranthus with velvety spikes stirring as if wakened to the proximities of blue agapanthus and plum-purple hollyhock and white lavaterra which were swaying at the side of silver grasses. She noticed, too, as she glanced inside the grove, how the recessions of light-reflected shadows overtook the vigorous ripple of tree colors there, disguising essential definitions of color and distance, too, so that space—welling backwards—darkened and disappeared within rising layers of dusk.

Everything about that day, in her retrospection at least, appeared disguised or dislocated. Even the wind seemed something other than itself. For when they'd paused on the emerald-rich hill leading to the sinuous path of the grove, she had believed just for an instant that the summery wind was the purest music, a melodious ornament of the air. Yet it was not the wind at all that she had heard or, rather, not the wind alone. She'd had to turn 'round, though, to discover the true-seeming source of the sound, allowing her gaze to move back to the banquet tables and sun-tinted people and back to festive images flowing in and out of the day's nebulous margins. Then, beyond those images, she saw once more the southwest corner of the Bradfords' main house. Its elegant Tudor ambiance wore exquisite shell carving along the gable trim, basketweave-and herringbone-patterned brick, and diamond-motif leaded windows. In that corner exuberant musicians orchestrated the convivial voices and self-reflective conversations of the guests (still sauntering along the banquet greenery) with the more mellifluous intonations of piano and violin, oboe and piccolo, trumpet and clarinet and tuba.

It was that confluence of sounds she had heard. The meld of resonating music and moody wind and pulsing human voices influenced—indeed, disguised—everything that she heard. Nothing was as it was alone. Each swelling timbre appropriated vibrancies other than its own and became something apart from and more than itself, concealed as it was within the melody of the wind and the hum of human voices and the lyrical harmonies of music.

From her implicated senses the day suppressed its accuracies, offering to her inquiring attention sights and sounds merely oblique in their truths, as if their essential reality were shunning the deepest layers of her comprehension. For the colors of the leaves were blemished by shadows in the grove. The music from the terrace was more than itself alone. Human voices floated inside soft cadences of wind. White, spumy waves tossed fitfully on the gentle-seeming ocean that flowed with glimmering ease below the hill where then she stood. And here—before her—Ryan Turner's laughing innocence flickered and gleamed like a temporary sun on the sea and just as quickly vanished. Yet each of these emblems of the day, these flourishing experiences of her senses, claimed a plausibility and justified an acceptance of the outward appearance of things.

With quiet confidence she had quickly accepted the outward appearance of things—all the palpable images of the iridescent earth and the suddenly flamingo clouds and the Prussian blue sea that had not yet reconciled themselves to the languorous drift of haze come to cover whole curvatures of space. Nor had she regarded as anything more than casual suggestion Ryan's apparently spontaneous remark that they—she and Steven—might enjoy standing upon the very promontory that had inspired the opening passages of the latest poem in a cycle which he had, for a year now, been composing.

They accepted his invitation because perhaps they wanted to retire discreetly, though only momentarily, from the gregarious fervor of that immense afternoon. Or possibly their furtive need for the unexpected persuaded them to join him. Or, more likely, their healthy pleasure in being drawn to the threshold of a young poet's imagination influenced them to peer for an instant upon the sensuous nature of his vision. His writerly skill enabled him to re-create the configurations of inlet and bay, grove and greenscape, festive sounds and flowered scents.

That Ryan Turner chose to express in poetic lines the vigorous narrative that was his life gave her soul-quickening pleasure. She had learned through wide travels with her parents and tutors and through voluminous reading in philosophy and history to associate authentic men, those charismatic ones who left their own firm imprints on the lacerating, rugged world, with keen-edged literary minds and self-willed heroic prowess. Her studies had, in fact, taught her to admire the youthful exuberance of Wordsworth in Paris scanning a momentous revolution, the burning wildness of Byron crying out to freedom at Missalonghi, and the prodigious Wilfred Owen daring to confront the stark blank sky at the Sambre Canal, knowing full well he had come to the end of the world.

To observe Ryan Turner whole and undiminished, his golden muscularity a summer radiance roused and compelling, was (she told herself) to witness manly assurance on the brink of new heroism and to recall once again the swiftly lived glories of those proven-brave poets. Whether he, too, would feel calm and original after the cleansing hour of rebellion or, risking all on a self-consuming deed, climb over the dark rim into early death, his steady eyes glazed in a face gone still and seraphic, only leavening time would finally disclose. But here, within the *now* that was this warm dissolving day, he seemed by himself alone a vivid justification for passion-wrought humanness.

"I want to find the hidden essence of things and of people," he told them confidently, as though confidence were the husky membrane of his potency. "There's adventure in that."

He had been explaining why, with its secret-furling winds and slanted whorls of light and shadows spun like wheels covering alcoves that surprised, he had chosen for the vista at the threshold of his poem a stalwart promontory which appeared to possess in full the summer-fragrant grove stirring behind it. In his eyes the promontory stood apparently indomitable while it waited for the sometimes-eddying sky and the dark, reeling waves of a storm-riven bay.

"This, I tell you, is a place where adventure should begin."

He held them carefully, Steven and even more so herself, inside that penetrating look of his that pulsed at the edge of what she regarded as a playful beckoning toward near-wildness. It was his promise of the unexpected and the surprise of her liking him so intensely which first put her off her proper course.

Yet even then, just before the festive afternoon wambled and tilted and whirled away from her control, she still consented to him as he dared her to thread her way unbaffled through his rapid processes. In that hour, while her heart toward him satisfied still with its gathering fullness, she had felt a tighter breathing rising fast from an unnoticed corner of her soul. This throbbing exhilaration he was drawing out of her was unanticipated evidence that in her especially there lived a splendid array of differences she had not yet tested, though they were so much more than the difference that was her safe demureness.

So it was that he had persuaded her (as if he were there alone beside her, murmuring his approval) to parry in a playful mode his spirited remark that the rugged promontory (where flashes of the dissolving afternoon sun vibrated like vaporous silver and where with them in seeming-casualness he stood) was an inspired place for finding a solid adventure. Before parrying his remark, she moved closer to Steven to clasp his large, athletic hands over the delicate touch of her own, so that all that she in that moment did or said seemed married to him alone. Only then did she speak the words that made her feel, in a rushing instant of newness, replenished and enlightened.

"We'll make an adventure for you, if you can't find one already here."

She saw at once that her brisk words awakened their keener awareness—her reliable Steven's, all earnest response and openness, and the far more complicated Ryan's, engendered as it was by his finely measured ambiguity. Through a language of hands answering the appealing promise of her vivid declaration, Steven clasped her ardently, as if this fluent motion of hands might leave upon her skin a permanent imprint of his heated body. But it was Ryan who gamely tossed her way the confident reply that called out to her desire to make an adventure.

"Feel free," he smoothly told her, his full, sensual lips once more in teasing union with a smile. That afternoon his resonating voice offered what she had accepted as a playful invitation. Hours later she would recognize it as the insidious challenge he had meant it to be—and he hardened and unflinching before the recoil of his words.

Now, in the press of desires no longer quiescent within her, his words were like wiry tendrils fastening their hold upon the secret senses inside her flesh, and not only his words, but his whole compelling presence. She accepted him entirely. She accepted, that is, the throbbing pulse of life he represented. While he was there all manly prowess before her, she seemed alone with him and complete in the sweep and push of that dissolving moment. Without waiting to feel herself lifted higher on the flow and arc of his tantalizing nearness or to ply him once more with witty retort or to attend the marrow and husk of her faithful Steven's briskness, she had to turn spontaneously and obliquely toward a remoter, far more steadying vision, her way of reclaiming a milder ease.

What she saw within the opaque-blue furling of distance, what directed her gaze to the floating pastel sky, was the umber ripple of a stray herring gull curving the dark flash of its wings against the tumescence of ponderous clouds. After an instant's pause, it plummeted with wily skill to the consenting lips of ocean water, the better to pluck for its meal a raw, ample fish or a tiny, mackerel-tinted seabird.

Though the vision gave her back what she had not sought, the imagery of danger shown natural and beautiful, she grasped comfortably its familiar message and found again her realistic measure for understanding things. Turning once more, still toward the east, she was not surprised to sight the zinc-white hang of wind-bleached cliffs glaring like the sea-tossed bones of a devoured world. She noticed, too, across and above quick Atlantic waters and on the crest of sun-glanced fertile hills—right there, at the wavering margins of the nebulous woods—a gray-blue immensity of swaying larches that apparently grew into the sky and, before her calmer eyes, joined all of heaven's restless and eerie motion.

She turned yet again, back to inspired and risk-taking Ryan standing before her and back to her essential Steven. Having so nearly reclaimed her composure, she could now permit herself to accept with concealed joy the full-bodied danger of Ryan's sensuality. Turning, she found once more what, despite her wakened need, she had not expected: the loop and list and swell of real adventure, like a dark, risen wave pitching upon them. This reckless Ryan and her rugged Steven, in extemporaneous league or seeming so, had devised a swaggering test of unbridled courage. They'd drawn up and sealed their casual pact in the brief moments she had looked away from their virile emphasis to reflect upon the wily laws of a hovering gull and the sea-anchored gravity of sullen, white cliffs and the arrogant powers of giant, majestic larches.

Their daring plan seemed to belong to both of them, so compatible with Ryan did Steven's sudden inclination toward risk make him. Yet it was Ryan, she surmised, who had first expressed the thought that, playful and unyielding, they should ride the wind-raked swell of the sea to test their fiercer capacities. During the previous week's lively regatta they had harnessed to the spirals of their own mastery the summer water's more temperate powers. That was a compelling reason to push themselves beyond the tight strictures of the ordinary. Racing against that afternoon's imminence of storm, they would confront with laughing camaraderie the sea's arduous, tangled restlessness. Or so, she learned upon turning back to them, Ryan had casually suggested. The even timbre of his affable words (she imagined later) modulated like sun-flecked shadows the glare of his hardened carelessness.

Their aim, he quickly explained once she had turned back to them, was to bring Steven's new, streamlined yawl into the afternoon's uneasy waters. Its vibrant-swift force would be poised against the sturdy, proven craft that Ryan intended to navigate. If the local Coast Guard station had issued prompt warning of the weather's uncertain temperament, that was not sufficient cause, Ryan said, for postponing what promised to be a lively competition. The race would be a realistic calculation of their seamanship and of the stamina of the boats whose speed they would command.

Call the experience an exhilarating complement to the day's festive atmosphere, he suggested, or a confident summoning of the courage required for a rapid skirmish with the sea or, perhaps, their conscious shaping of an episode worth the telling in his poem. Call it, they must, as they liked, he shrugged before both of them now, moments after she had turned back to them. But they should not, through a habit of safer propensities, forfeit the pulsing capacity they held within themselves—each of them—for venturing bravely into the immense world's shifting possibilities.

Ryan spoke as if for all of them. Yet she understood at once that his words, a brisk way to glance at self-defeating reticence, were meant for her alone. For long ago, she suspected, he had left behind with laughing disdain the hesitation that stymies or trammels brave-hearted enterprise. In these few weeks of their knowing him, he had already witnessed Steven's capacity to confront the unknown without the circumspection that too cautiously measures probability, the over-refined analysis that diminishes or deflects both force and originality. Sailing in a formidable regatta, he and Steven together had winningly demonstrated the symmetry and sweep of authentic daring. So it was she toward whom he had just then directed the vigor and shape of his words.

Because, perhaps, he meant to validate her intuition, he held her firmly, as though they alone were there together, within the throb and tension of his gaze.

"You're joining us, of course," he told her. His self-assurance generated quite naturally the coiling rhythms into which he was drawing her.

If she paused, it was only for an instant, to tally the cost to her safe ease of his startling invitation. Then, casting aside all her familiar reckonings and most of her misgivings, she accepted the freefall into his challenge.

"What a grand idea," she found herself saying. The sheer pleasure of being in dangerous flight with him was new and exotic.

But no sooner had she done so, no sooner had she entered without open chute or ballast of any other kind the thrilling plunge into all that he was offering her, than she looked with delicate inquiry toward Steven. It had become her habit to interpret through his studious eyes her subtle effect upon a scene. How often she had sought out and found among a mingling concourse of guests and during their brightest repartee his beaming consent to whatever words or gestures she had chosen for that moment to define herself. She had sought out, as well, amidst graver matters, when she in his presence was able to stand reliably alone before the lacerating betrayals of a day's serener promises, his quiet approval that held at bay the show of every response except civility.

Today, though, when the stillness that held Steven's features tight came now to watch with him her curious alterations, he offered her neither consent nor dismay. His was the courtesy that quietly beholds the different tint or sudden, complicated traceries of a young woman's character. So long, or so it seemed, did he pause inside his stillness, so fraught with anticipation did he render her art of waiting, that without receiving his assenting expression or the vibrant reply which, though unaware of how much he gave her, would tell her he had not noticed her sinuous yearning for Ryan, she spoke the thought that broke the spell his silence was casting upon them.

"Oh, Steven," she declared with affecting optimism. "We're going to have such a splendid time."

But even now, in the genteel sight of her influence that was (she permitted herself to imagine) like no other influence upon him except, perhaps, her cool, reviving touch or fragrant-soft elegance, he stood as one alone within the pensive shadings of his stillness. He held his ruddy lips firmly together in some honest covenant or studious alliance that shaped from a smile's vestige and the moment's anchoring stillness a sturdy young man's discomforting apprehension. Though he might from time to time, as an invigorating release from obligations wound like a tight shroud about him, welcome into his own life the perilous unraveling of chance, he saw (apart from the charm of it) her desire to be one with him and with Ryan as well in their plan to soar—reckless and proprietary—above foam-capped waves and clouded, swirling waters as the folly of unjustified risk.

Whether Steven would from that day regard as a similar folly his own forays inside the stark cusp and thrilling clasp of dangerous chance, she (hearing later of all that happened in these hours) did not care to guess, so elliptical and varied were the stories generated by this misadventure of the boating party. Well-schooled as he was, however, in his privileged family's traditions, Steven would have learned, as an essential law of manly honor, that he must do all that could be done to protect a woman from the world's ungoverned harms and sometimes, if need be, from herself. On that July afternoon, then, he may have found no inconsistency between his reluctance to allow her a polite dallying with an imminence of stormy waters and his more serious enthusiasm for launching himself upon the colored flares of perilous time. The race on the sea would be a fiercer way for a promising lawyer to cauterize his wounded senses against a walled-in life of corporate litigation and test as well his most formidable capacities, unused and even buried since his heroic time in the recent war with Germany.

It was, in fact, a formidable test that he and Ryan had devised. For them, a willful race on restless waters made absolute sense, because they brought to their knowledge and love of the sea a joyful athleticism. Theirs was a poised and accurate proficiency that hones its muscular aptitudes on realistic self-appraisal. Not for them the unruly, self-defeating bravado that lacks both wit and mastery. Instead, they claimed an unflinching awareness of the precise radius of their youthful powers and, better still, a respectful apprehension of the monumental sea. That she, with her ethereal perception of things, should want to join them (in what she deemed exotic pastime as easily abandoned as begun) brought him to a sober pause and a nebulous margin of disquiet that Ryan could so casually invite her to the astonishing onrush of risk.

She watched Steven hold himself inside that pause. His rugged demeanor offered still no other sign but coolheaded observation. His was a keen strategy for clarifying an ambiguous moment and arriving at the path on which he might courteously deflect his elegant young lady's compelling idea. So intrigued did he seem by the charm of it and so roused was his reflective glance upon her, that she noticed only gradually the nearly imperceptible reserve that keeps approving words at bay.

It was Ryan, instead, who first recognized his summer friend's lingering introspection as the silent language of reluctance. Impatient by then that they should, nonetheless, hurry on to the afternoon's quickening vibrancies, he spoke the clipped thought that meant to call reliable Steven away from his swift mind's assailing realism.

"You're still game, aren't you?" he asked.

The drift of his words carried a challenge more than a question.

His good-natured ease appearing to return, Steven eyed him more carefully. It was with ungrudging admiration that he studied this tall, lithe arrogance who defined his nature with subtle persuasion, here on a glimmering promontory.

"Why not?"

His words expressed the confidence that he was bringing to the race on the sea awaiting them.

"We'll make a dash for it and, win or lose, have a bit of excitement."

Ryan grinned, a flash of approval tempering the penetrating gaze that said he would hold Steven to his promise.

Hearing this prospect of excitement spoken in the ocean air as though it were an invocation to a playful fury of waters, she smiled her soft exhilaration, still safe and properly modulated.

But the thought he wanted most to convey Steven had not yet declared. So he went forward, finding the words that, after a pause, meant to eclipse this sudden plan that she would join them in their risk.

"The race is between you and me," he told Ryan. "Having Linda with me would be an unfair advantage, because she knows enough about sailing to be a winning partner."

A flicker of Ryan's attention noticed even as it abandoned her wistful demureness. Instead, he accepted face-to-face the full measure of strong-minded Steven, whose sober calm was directing him with apparent effortlessness to a strategy for protecting his fiancée from the day's possible folly. It was then that Ryan sought to disarm his summer friend's waiting protest.

"Oh, the race will be a fair one, no doubt about that," he replied, as if in good faith he were encouraging a fellow athlete, "and we'll be evenly matched."

He saw at once how, with muted surprise, the two of them, Steven and her, stood watching him now with a tighter stillness. But only after he'd turned away from the silver-blue vision of the sea and began walking toward the shadowy edge of the grove did he pause to look back upon them and with crisp affability dispel the moment's mystery.

"We'll be very evenly matched," he said, as though in repetition he might exorcise their new uncertainty and find his way to an enjoyable admission. "After all," he added, his eyes gleaming with what afterwards they told themselves was an amused wiliness, "I'll also have a winning partner."

Though his remark stirred their tentative surprise, they allowed him no other evidence of unease or even the crimson flush of dismay that rises before thoughts of friendship's subtle pledges return to calm and irrigate the senses. So fascinated were they still by his propensity for the unexpected, so proficient was his serpentine maneuvering with chance, that they held unspoken, within the coherent patterns of their courtesy, the brisk question which could draw forth the identity of this winning partner.

Now, without a word to cancel or affirm the verve of their summer bond with him, they (as if compelled by their silent inquiry) followed Ryan along the sloping path that paused discreetly at the edge of the grove. For a moment she imagined that Steven's brother Aaron, with a blunt sufficiency as self-absorbed as it was pragmatic, had decided to test his own athletic prowess in league with a school-mate who courted with arrogant charm all manner of dangerous possibilities.

But when they returned to the fragrant entrance of the grove, berberis and verbena still glowing with blushed motion beside the fragile whiteness of lavaterra and the wakened shimmer of silver grasses, they at first looked in vain for this mysterious partner. She supposed reasonably that Aaron, all supple brawn and honed-sharp energy, would have skillfully eluded any further contact with his family's elegant summer party and arrived with brusque confidence for the launching of this rugged skirmish with the sea. Only the billowing wind had arrived, though, like a flare of wings lifted by lower winds and pushing upward now against moist, sea-scented air.

This feeling of space actively stirring, this sense that there on a sun-hued promontory the wind had come sweeping through the day's intricate layers and, spinning always its rapid coils, had come to claim them—it was this feeling that stopped their firm gait suddenly and held them in taut surprise back upon their heels while cliffs and clouds and festive summer colors went wheeling by them. The earth itself seemed to revolve with visible motion. She noticed once more the receding diagonals of the grove—a shadow-flecked welling of foliage and trees, an instant's ambiguity of surface and space. She noticed too Ryan's careful scrutiny of that same sequestered place.

Only then did she see her hurrying out of the darkness toward them. Her flowing blonde hair and alabaster radiance granted her the spectral look of a mirage or an apparition. Now, while whorls of slanted light began cautiously to receive her, Linda saw who she was and, seeing, understood, with no need of words to declare or clarify, that her sister, Tracy, was the mysterious partner whom Ryan had chosen.

Though Tracy offered them the courtesy of a charming smile, it was Ryan to whom she gave her excited words.

"Quinn has everything ready," she said. Her voice with Ryan already intimated (or so Linda at once suspected) the hold he had upon her sister.

If a smoldering glance can sometimes convey, as the world's philosophers of feverous love have told us, the heated properties of a sensual embrace, then Ryan had surely enfolded, with the ardor of a burnished look, both body and soul of this willowy girl hurrying toward him as toward a pleasure of the heart. What Linda first saw when her sister emerged from the wind-roused grove was sun-misted light scattering the darkness that hovered about her. Then, but only for a moment, she perceived something altogether astonishing. It was as though her eyes had just then discovered their capacity for divining nature's hidden likenesses—the sudden affinities that shape our new awareness of existing things. For the sun-touched shadow Ryan's vigorous presence cast upon her sister looked so like a looming wave rising to claim her and lifting the ground from under her feet.

"We're ready, too," he casually remarked.

Turning now, he led them away from the grove's fruit-scented threshold. There, flame-orange blooms of potentilla and chestnut-red irises and warm coppery-pink chrysanthemums went on swaying in sensuous ease. He led them as well away from a summer party's evanescent human voices and mellifluous violas and flutes and bassoons and furling surges of the sun-dappled bay. From the comforting southern corner behind them, the heady, resonating wind still wafted sea-and-flower fragrances. Onto the graveled path he brought them, guiding them all the while toward new melodies of wind and waters and to the boat house where old, duty-bound Quinn, the grizzled attendant, waited. It was he whom Ryan had privately directed (she surmised, on hearing Tracy's exhilarated words) to prepare two boats for launching.

Quinn's gruff heartiness and cynical enjoyment of the unexpected would, she knew from first-hand experience, quicken his willingness to carry out Ryan's directive.

Not without his own appreciation of Ryan's unorthodox devices for subverting the humdrum and familiar, Steven (she sensed) found himself resenting nonetheless, just a little, the younger man's proprietary maneuvering of their day. Perhaps he really meant that afternoon to thwart this wild youth's plan to parry with the restless sea. With his own brisk confidence he hurried along the glimmering path, a haze like blue flax already rising to encoil them. Placing his large, athletic hand on his new friend's shoulder, Steven persuaded him to pause.

"You're very sure of us," he said, his words held firm inside a tighter huskiness.

No sooner had he spoken, than they, he and Ryan, studied each other with a keen steadiness. A soldierly stillness allowed them time to gather the sum of each other's meaning. Now, as if to declare the language by which they could in affable fraternity go forward, Ryan chose the agreeable words that would keep them on their course.

"I'm sure of all my friends," he said, a flicker of a smile tracing his matter-of-factness.

Was that the moment when she might have, by speaking honest words, saved them all from the unhappy excitement that followed? Was it then that she might have saved all of them by choosing to utter an uncomplicated language that resisted Ryan's undermining their safe priorities?

(For weeks afterwards Linda wondered, while remembering the apparent playfulness of that festive afternoon, which only in retrospect seemed colored falsely, like a tinted sky concealing immensities of storm.)

But she did not speak the precise words that might have held all of them to their proper course. Without anything but the compass of affection to guide us into new, exuberant fellowship, how does the heart measure accurately the motives of another human being? She had accepted Ryan, as she had accepted Steven. With their careful breeding and aristocratic textures, they were in different ways extraordinary. Each of them was a dynamic presence, inviting her to broaden, and perhaps deepen, the enigmatic circumference of herself—the always-changing, mysterious perimeters of her never-completely-charted nature. No, she did not speak the proper words that might have saved all of them. She had no art to decipher the unknown or to guess that a playful boat race on the sea and its abrasive aftermath would be sufficient occasion for disarranging their lives and making grievous recollection a constant, visible scene.

Steven, though, had meant to speak out. With levelheaded inquiry, he approached this enterprising youth whom he had come to regard as a secret blood brother or foster spirit reflecting his own life-quickening capacities. But he yielded the moment, nevertheless, to whatever plan that chance or fate or willful Ryan or she herself cared to impose upon a restless summer day.

Some might say that it was she, not arbitrary fate or random chance or wily Ryan, who now influenced the yet-alterable pattern their casual day without much notice was weaving. It was she who arrived at the secluded spot where Steven and Ryan were conferring. There in the blue haze of the sun-tinged graveled path, she delicately touched her fiancé's rugged arm. Quite naturally he looked her way and, noticing her elated eyes, comprehended without a word or any gesture other than the graceful touch of her fingers the currents of her quiet desire.

If she influenced the pendulous swing of that moment, it was perhaps the cool touch of her fingers upon Steven's heated skin and the elated glow of her eyes that moved him to speak the very words his canny judgment had meant to withhold from the festive afternoon which all of a sudden, an hour or so later, would pitch and slope away from them.

"You've a mind for sailing," he said, with a clipped directness that made his simple language sound vigorous and original.

She in turn smiled a discreet assent, her words held still in silence. Only a poised, nearly imperceptible nod affirmed her reply.

"Then we'll sail," he jauntily beamed, "though the four of us will, I think, be racing mainly the weather."

Her satisfied heart allowed her to answer this time with unrestrained clarity.

"We'll have a marvelous time."

Perhaps it was the prospect of an afternoon's swift sport on the sea which satisfied her, or Steven's enthusiasm for her quiet desire, which he chose to interpret not as a passing whim, but an ardent need. Just as possibly it was the stir of pleasure she felt in deflecting her disarranged expectation that she alone would be the woman soaring recklessly with Ryan through the temporary afternoon.

Or, more likely, it was her clear-sighted though uneasy awareness of how the day's indirections had delivered her from herself. A sometime familiar stranger to herself, she had allowed this wild youth, this subtle cruelty called Ryan Turner, to take hold of her mind and spirit for an hour or two and then, as sated with her as if he had claimed her physically as well, to turn indifferently away.

Whether it was any one of these things which saved or satisfied her or only some of them or none at all, she did not know. While from time to time silently recounting that day, she never fully clarified herself to herself, intuiting perhaps that none of us can parcel out our motives by geometric rules or split our desires like a territory coiling into round or perpendicular.

As if her words were a promise that the rising trees and whirl of winds and wheels over wheels of summer-bay waters would excite the slanting afternoon just enough to exhilarate their senses and give a boat race on a tilting sea a surge of safer peril, they hurried down to the waiting dock and gleaming yawls and gnarled curmudgeon Quinn.

His mumbled inflections were both warning and solicitude that he directed toward all of them and toward Steven most of all, for Quinn had served the Bradfords for thirty years and more.

"There's a stronger wind behind this one, Mr. Bradford."

"A strong wind's what we have in mind, Quinn," Steven asserted with a boldness that enjoys itself. "Today we're going to ride her."

So confident did Steven seem, so caught up was he by this billowing energy of the unexpected, that self-willed Ryan, for the last minute or so having consented to the convolutions of his own observing stillness, called out to them with typical ease, as though his spoken thought were by itself a vigor that would prevail over the swerving chances of that hour.

"Now we'll have a real adventure," he said.

No sooner had he done so than they heard, as an ancillary influence or perhaps an independent power, Tracy's impassioned elation. Her words, as Steven and she remembered them afterward, were yearning and still innocent, a romantic girl's heartfelt and wistful hope.

"We'll have days and days of adventure," she said. "We'll have whole years of happiness."

While she spoke, descending with them the path to the jetty and the waiting boats, she whirled about as in a dance. She was a graceful flowing of summer garments and golden hair.

As she perceived her, Tracy appeared to be confirming, rather than claiming as new, the full-bodied colors of her nature. In her eyes, the joyous rush of imagery that on this day her sister represented was but one of a hundred plausible variations of the person that she already was. It might have been, as well, a suppressed or evolving version of herself she had not sufficiently tested.

She had in these few weeks of her family's visit with the Bradfords, here within this luminous seascape that so admirably quickened the senses, impressed her as someone ancillary or incidental to the life-loving and effectual girl that she had been before their mother died. It was as if, by collaborating with their father's grief, she was learning to live with stinted powers.

Once, while she and Steven sauntered barefoot by the sea, along early morning's gleaming white sand that waited to be touched by the sinuous ripples of sun-flecked waters, they saw Tracy coming toward them from out of a mist-shrouded distance. Her willowy grace stood not alone, but in lingering consonance with her father, as if reluctant to travel away from his tightly wrought sorrow. Later, on an afternoon when they were returning from their own sauntering along the path that glided beside the shimmering meadow behind the west wing of the house, they watched her from afar. Alone then, she was lovely in a white-flowing cotton dress and an azure parasol. Strolling along the deserted beach, she was looking out over the wide expanse of a restless sea, compelled by a vision they had not yet apprehended.

It was only when she moved too quickly toward the breaking waves that for an instant they believed she was going to drown herself. Calling her name in apprehensive voices that fell beneath the crash of the breakers and inside the restless winds, they ran across the space that separated her from them. But when they reached her willowy form, they received an altogether different impression. She had (they told themselves) stepped back from the sea and now wore a look of surprise that the breaking waves had wet her dress. Caught as she was within her weary unhappiness, she had not realized that she was walking so dangerously close to the sea.

When she turned to them, aware now that they had hurried there to watch her with curious eyes, she gently took their hands into hers. She seemed grateful that they stood so protectively beside her.

"The sea is restless today," she said. "That's when I love it most of all. It tells me that my restlessness may be a natural thing, too."

She sensed the tension in her sister. Her careful voice could not conceal the fact that she had been crying.

Steven noticed, too. With easy courtesy, he offered her words meant to call her away from her sorrow.

"Let's be restless together," he said. "I'm sure that you, Linda, and I can find an adventure or two during these next weeks."

Almost imperceptibly, she held his hand more firmly. Her tearful eyes brightened momentarily. But her lips could not compose the affectionate smile she had often given him so easily.

Influenced by Steven's sympathetic manner, she began coaxing Tracy away from her brooding.

"Mother wouldn't want you to grieve like this," she told her. "She would want you to make the best of things."

Tracy paused, as if she were weighing the realism of the thought.

"How can I, when Father is so unhappy?"

"Your father will put this hard time behind him," Steven said. "You must do the same."

She paused again. Then, with reluctant words that were soft at first and tremulous, she addressed the both of them through new tears.

"I wish I could be like Father," she lamented. "I wish I could love Mother as he does, as though she were alive and with us."

Before this sight of her grieving sister, she took pause. Older than Tracy by seven years and away at private schools and, afterward at Bryn Mawr, she had been, for the most part, unavailable as the helpful counselor and nurturing friend she would surely have chosen to be, had there not been so wide a disparity between their ages and had their daily activities put them more in the way of each other. Not even when she returned home to help care for her dying mother did she find herself in her sister's presence, for Tracy herself was then away at school. In those rare times when they *were* in each other's company, she tried to be a friend to her. But she had sensed that Tracy, always polite and often lighthearted, preferred to keep her at a distance. She associated her, perhaps, with the grown-ups whom she regarded as authority figures rather than as friends.

From time to time she had been very pleased to notice her sister conversing affably with others on the sun-glanced terrace of their Newport home—their father perhaps or one of the Norwegian or Chinese girls who attended her school and, as a guest in their seaside residence for a month or so, was sharing with the family summer's lighthearted activities. But on one occasion, when she had entered the library without expecting to find anyone there, she met the somber pensiveness of her sister, coiled as she was within its traces. On a different afternoon she had observed her too-still quietude in the shadowy light of the drawing room window from which she was wistfully peering. Only on those days had she noticed what, later, Steven would tell her he also had perceived. A tincture of sadness was enshrouding Tracy's bright surfaces. There was in her a nearly imperceptible suggestion of private sorrow and a tint of weariness, sequestered and momentary.

Steven remembered that in previous years Tracy had been life-loving and exuberant. In those days all of the Maguires, including their mother, had from their own neighboring home summered with the Bradfords as a family whole and integral. Always, Tracy inspirited a scene with her quick-witted and affable nature.

To observe her in these recent weeks of his knowing her once more, however, was to receive her not as herself or as a total stranger even, but as someone altogether unexpected. She was somebody different, if not completely separate—a reflection of a vital girl he felt he had known and accurately remembered. The imagery of herself in full bloom now told his apprehension none the less who she used to be and taught his eyes to receive her as a distinctive counterpart to the happy girl he remembered seeing from time to time with her parents before the war. To his present glance, the anguish that she held within herself was an authentic part of her essence. This additional layer of her existence had only in these summer weeks disclosed itself to his sudden capacity for seeing within the imagery that was herself exactly as he had anticipated someone revised for his comprehension.

Yet never—not even in these hard months after their mother's death—had Tracy of her own volition revealed to her by outward sign or shared confidence any unhappiness or dismay, except perhaps for the tears a young girl sometimes sheds because of a day's fleet disappointment. For that reason, she—being a discreet older sister—resolved never to intrude upon so intricate a process as her sister's individuality. But always she maintained toward her a warm and earnest demeanor, as spontaneous as it was decorous. Had her sister ever called out to her for encouragement or assistance or rescue of any kind, she would have gladly and effectually answered. But Tracy had never called out to her. It was only now, in the roused uneasiness of a wind-swept afternoon, that she had quite by chance apprehended the truth of her sister's deep-rooted sorrow. Only now, without intending to do so, did her sister call to her and call as clearly to Steven.

"I want to be happy again," she said as they walked with her back to the house. "I want to feel free of all care, because it is summer and I am young."

"We'll help you find your way back to yourself," Steven told her. "We'll show you how to be happy again."

His husky friendliness ignited brotherly capacities, and the affection in his glance brought the hint of a smile to her lips.

"For the rest of this summer," she assured her sister, "you are going to enjoy everything."

In the weeks that followed, she and Steven orchestrated days and days of happiness for her. Always, they drew to her an enthusiastic company of athletic youths and poised young ladies who had become her loyal friends through the years. At times, other parents joined her and Steven as chaperones who kept themselves at a respectful distance that allowed Tracy and her friends a proper latitude for navigating their individuality.

As a life-loving group, they first kayaked along the Sakonnet River in nearby Tiverton. There, after paddling to Blue Bell Cove just west of the river's basin, they explored the picturesque islands and beaches. In Sakonnet Point a few days later, they journeyed on their bicycles through a rambling scenic trail. It was a lift to their spirits, upon reaching the village of Little Compton, to ride past the expansive wetlands and pastures.

During the following week, as exuberant as ever, the group visited a farm on Aquidneck Island that recalled an eighteenth-century Swiss Village. As though they had entered a long-ago past, they traversed its thirty-two acres in 1840 Seabrook Carriages that were pulled by American Cream draft horses. All around them they saw green, undulating pastures, rugged and ample trees, and sun-glistening ponds. Behind the main house, which was constructed of rough-cut rock that had been blasted out of the surrounding ledge, rhododendron bushes soared to generous heights. They saw as well, in pastures some distance from the home field, Randall Lineback cattle, Belted Galway cows, Florida cracker horses, Tennessee Myotonic goats, and Gulf Coast sheep. Irregular stone bollards kept horses and carriages on the pebble roadway that went winding through the farm. Occasionally, an exotic bird sauntered by a pond or chose a guardrail as its resting place.

From her perch in a carriage with Steven and with the engaging Morrisons, whose son and daughter were among the most gregarious in the group, she could see Tracy and her peers in a carriage that was hurrying just ahead of their own. Neal and Carolyn Morrison were there with her, and so was Ryan Turner. In that moment it cheered her to see Tracy looking buoyant and receptive as she shared lighthearted anecdotes with her friends.

Most memorable of all their excursions, so Tracy told her and Steven afterward, was their climb to Ferry Cliff in Bristol County. On that day their group included only six persons. Besides Steven, Tracy and her, there were Ryan Turner and the young Morrisons—Neal and Carolyn. During these hours, Ryan appeared to give far more attention to the Morrison girl than to Tracy. It was Neal Morrison who actively courted her sister's interest. To him she responded with an easy blitheness.

But only intermittently had she noticed her sister and the others.

Instead, she gave herself almost completely to the new experience of climbing to the highest ridge that peered over Bristol Harbor. There, just beyond the nest of a white-eared hummingbird and beyond windswept tufts of grass, she saw and heard—as for the first time because so near her and actual—the quickened wing-beat of a herring gull. With Steven on that same ridge, she also observed the sun resting on a bank of clouds where its light shone brighter and more neutral. A ghostly mist disturbed the hill below them and touched as well the sailboats and ships that were leaving or returning to the harbor. In that moment she perceived in a different way the curving surfaces of the sea.

"You've brought me to life again," Tracy told Steven and her one morning a few days afterward. They had just enjoyed a brisk swim in the Bradfords' cantilevered pool that flowed into the waters of the Atlantic. "I have never been so happy."

"The summer will be with us for many weeks," she told her. "Steven and I are planning other special days for you and your friends."

"We promised you a good time," Steven said, "and we intend to keep our word."

Her sister was delighted at the prospect of being with them and with her friends.

"I had almost forgotten all the wonderful and familiar things that can make me happy."

Hearing her elated words, she and Steven were very pleased. They had rescued her from all her sorrow. They had shown her how to call back the self she had lost after their mother's death.

Now, four weeks later, they were heartened once more to find that she was joining them in the day's unexpected flare of surprise. Her bright anticipation brought them a new pleasure. Surely, this boat race over restless waters would satisfy her need to be in the world, new and self-reliant and evolving.

2

So they sailed into the unfurling wind, receiving it still as a gift for their senses. It was both echoing melody and wafting sea-fragrance. It was elusive caress and cloud-driving impetus. Already the sky was discarding its cerulean textures and revealing with incautious spontaneity bruised grays and violets and crimsons. But the dazzle and warm lilt of that late afternoon shimmered yet across their youthful spirits. Still it dispensed the crispness of its favor and betrayed none of its promise for their venture-laden expectations.

Linda remembered that first hour on the bay as a series of indirections and a discovery of unexpected inclines and sinuous turnings. It seemed in the sheer lift and pulse of her enthusiasm as though they, in their sailboats leaving the shore, were disengaging themselves from essential roots and anchors and foundations. That fleet portion of the world unfurling before her heart-quickened senses was all disengagement and even dislocation. It was a swift disjoining of earth's safer boundaries not only from the intricate transitions of the bay, but from the ballast and equilibrium of the familiar, as well.

There, beyond the brine-green wake of waters whose roiling track glistened on the brisk sea's disarrangement—right there, while before the lilt and glow of her backward glance the shoreline in rapid motion eluded with an agile geometry the summer waves' wily incursions— just there, at the sun-glanced line where the furrowing sea arced toward the shore, the land leaped, tensile and accurate and then swerved and spun and scrolled, scattering whole houses and trees and summer people. Or so it seemed to her excited senses.

So it seemed as with comfortable acumen she eased the yawl's white-flashing jibsheets to test the wind's new, supple currents and afterwards, as her limber Steven with synchronous powers taught the mainsail to scan both risk and necessity. So to her it all so marvelously seemed in the thrill and push of her flourishing awareness that this wayward afternoon could find its meaning in their unexpected departure from the land and in their undeclared surrender of all the places that knew them. It found its meaning as well in their leave-taking of the selves they had so often compassed and, paradoxically, in their willful arrival before the convoluted mysteries of the sea and before their own mysteries and convolutions.

Now, while turning toward wind-raveling waters and sun-clasped clouds and the floating haze of chrome green hills across the bay, she noticed—as though he were a prowess as intricate as the sea—magnificent Ryan Turner. He was hiking out over the gunwales of his craft, his ruggedness tethered by canvas straps to his yawl's brisk velocity. Vivid and actual, he was in her approving eyes like the sun-gold youth from nautical stories taming a wily dolphin or like some unknown sea-god with a mind for balancing a sailboat as well as ocean winds and waters. And there beside Ryan while hiking with him to windward was exhilarated Tracy. Leaning assured and proprietary into hastening space just beyond their heeling vessel, she appeared at that very instant to be rising from foam-covered waves glancing off their boat's zinc-white hull.

Impossible it was to keep but a moment, in the surging awareness of her senses, this imagery of Tracy and

Ryan as confident allies of the day's rapid processes. So smoothly did they bring their craft to a confluent swiftness and balance that the burnished imagery that was themselves navigating their vessel hastened into the sun-flecked recessions of space before her, where the blue-opal distance kept spiraling backward. So much brighter than day were they to her eyes on that occasion that even the sea appeared to part its vigorous waters. It was as if for them alone together, for daring Ryan and vital Tracy, there grew voluminous and tactile a faster corridor hurrying them away from the lift and flare of her fleeting glance toward a territory of bold cutters and catboats, a half-dozen or more, glimmering above the churning push of darker waters.

But farther than that even, though before the pulsing skyline sloped and spun within a haze of hills—just before— there, on wind-flung waves and teeming mist, a solitary yawl rippled like flickering light, gold-orange and amber and viridian silver. Then, because new radiance above the yawl directed her attention, she saw a cadre of glaucous-winged gulls pursuing hidden curvatures of sunlight and air and rose-tinted cloud. Only minutes after that, in the flurrying distance, she glimpsed inlet and bay, greenscape and grove, and the silver-blue sheen of a promontory. Yet sometimes she understood—in an instant—glint of meadow and gleam of farm-field and congregant trees stirring like celestial bodies. Suddenly, even then in that race across the bay, she knew again as palpable and actual the hard-bodied whiteness of a waiting lighthouse. And always, while with her rugged Steven she became on rapid waters a collateral emphasis, she felt summer-warm winds spilling around them as from a sail of the quick, mysterious earth.

But the wind, aromatic still with sweet-bitter scent of ruckled waters and land-spawned flower fragrances, occasionally held back its sea-driving favor. At the very moment that Ryan and Tracy hurried past them, beyond the swift recoil of waking waters, the wind with blunt surprise struck their sails, hers and her athletic Steven's, on the lee side. It enclosed them within its torpid shadow (what mariners call the blanket zone) and annulled at once their boat's nimble powers. Held aloft, with tension poised, their sails waited.

No sooner had Ryan, all the while racing with furious ease, deflected the wind's force away from Steven's sail, than with his own formidable seamanship inspiriting him Steven trimmed his boat's mainsheet close-hauled. Only afterwards, when the forward edge of his sail began to ripple, did he find a proper path for making his way out of the imprisoning blanket zone into a soaring vigor that was freedom once more and new-claimed velocity. Then his craft knew boundlessness horizontal and leaping and knew as well curving verticality, so often leaning and sometimes precarious.

So in this swifter flash of late afternoon did she and Steven approach again the fluency that was Ryan and Tracy sailing across the hastening span of the sea. But never could they surpass them or gain a leeward power to send a stalling backwind upon them. Yet how vigorously and with supple acumen did Steven pilot their vessel's bold maneuverings. She herself activated the adventure with him. She with him kept riding the crest of hurling chance—and they together a brave and ardent reciprocity. Rarely had exhilaration for them together been as supreme as in that billowing hour of risk. Awareness became a crisper form of breathing as when they two, navigating a momentous soaring of the senses, a surging of will and pulse and aptitude, noticed—as a mirror of their own becoming—Ryan and Tracy riding across space and time so fearlessly. For the wind-whipped bucking world, its sea and land and altitude as well, was theirs to test and tame and possess, at least for a flourishing sun-gold season.

Once again this brave imagery of Ryan and Tracy rising over the crest of luminous waters glanced back at their apprehension, hers and Steven's, and hurried onward, as if the radiance in which they rode belonged to them alone and only they were their parallel. Yet even together Ryan Turner and Tracy Maguire were each of them a self distinct and italic. Their individuality remained buoyant and whole all the while they were so joyously there together. Only obliquely did they surrender the identity that separately was each of them, intrinsic.

It was the clarity of this recognition that heartened her. For it validated her earlier intuition that she and Steven, married, would be a fusion of so many evolving identities. They would be infinite-seeming versions and revisions of their differences and of their mutuality. How wonderful, she'd thought, to be alive and young and original, even as one's self enfolded another—even as one's soul and spirit and always-quickened mind embraced the pulse and throb of existence as a discovery absolutely new—experience inwoven and singular.

Now it was that she declared, because the wily day had shown her the danger that was in herself, the sheer thrill of ascending the curve and slope of that afternoon with catapulting chance beside her.

"There's so much adventure here, and we are a part of it," she told Steven as he stood by the tiller, looking toward the blue-green margins of the horizon. Hearing her words, he turned to her reflectively. Then with an assured muscularity he reached out to caress her shoulder, as if by a lover's touch he could enter whatever new mystery was welling within her.

He laughed a deep-hearted laugh, easing his way into her elation, and then spoke the thought that was as a fuse to her excitement.

"*We* are the adventure."

So it seemed to their excited senses. So, even and especially in the last rapturous moments of their race on the bay, it all so wonderfully seemed while the wily day, glimmering now within intricacies of mist, cast a spectral glow upon them and upon everything they could see. The whole of reality, or at least the portion of the world which they together were beholding, seemed to disappear gradually. Perhaps (she mused) the oblique surrender of identity was a fundamental law not only of adventure, but of everything else that was coherent and plausible and apparently real.

Still they apprehended the light and colors of exhilaration. Still they could see in the rapid distance before them the flare of yawls and catboats and cutters. From time to time they discovered, fearless and exuberant, Ryan and Tracy riding on the crest of new venturing. Sun-fused clouds went on waiting and the ample sky leaned, languorous and approving, upon playful, iridescent waters. All the while, as the greenery of the land leaped and the ambivalent shoreline swerved, she with her accomplished Steven reveled at the very rim of that day's taut harmonies.

Then the afternoon turned to other purposes. The air glowed with lightning-flame. Its gash of orange-yellow and eerie glaze of umber and green gave notice of impending wildness. Roused suddenly, winds pushed away whole alliances of clouds, gone dark-bruised gray and indigo. The sky billowed, disarranged as the bay rose and cascaded. Space—welling backward—disappeared within curves of haze and on the roiling timbres of thunder and, just as suddenly, returned to align itself with familiar outlines of day. New light erupted from a pearl-gray vortex of clouds, saturating hills and sky and sea and covering as well sailboats that leaned more than rode upon pulsing waters.

That was the storm's enigmatic harbinger for the next half-hour or more, while late afternoon, understanding perhaps the strategies of storm, fulfilled ordinary obligations and waited.

How long the storm would wait, ambivalently reconciled with its stinted powers, neither she nor Steven paused to guess. For there had been, valued and remembered, other days in their experience of the sea when wind and wave and velocity, each of them reconnoitering and inflective, had held back their assailing powers temporarily. Only then did shafts of sunlight and rich vitalities of color gradually return to reconstruct what had so swiftly been dislocated or dispelled or lost even: the more affable sensations of summer's reality vibrant over sail-worthy waters. How, after all, when the storm had already shown its belligerent features, could pausing avail them or any other boatman riding those uncertain waters? No, they did not pause to guess at the sea's imminent heft and swell and turbulent ascensions. Instead, with a mariner's gift for interpreting the weather's equivocal language and with her in mind first of all, Steven resolved that he must pilot his craft away from the storm's waiting powers.

"We'll go back," he calmly told her.

A skillful sailor herself needing no other explanation, she smiled in quick-witted agreement. (They, both of them, were a bright splendor in sun-gold oilskins and with the energy of knowledgeable motion.)

So, easing the tiller slowly and rounding up into a favorable wind, he brought his craft skillfully about. After trimming flat and relying now on his storm sail alone, he began the journey homeward.

Still the storm withheld for a time its wilder capacities while, proficient and exhilarated yet, they sailed by way of Dyer Island, to the Bradfords' estate near Brenton Point. It was wonderful then, and more so than at the start of their race, to see in the opaque-blue furling of distance the floating pastel sky. They could see as well, soaring on gleaming curve and flash, the vigorous whiteness of herring gulls and near the crest of viridian clouds—or seeming so—the gray-blue immensity of swaying larches. More palpable than those because nearer and emphatic, hills and cliffs and farm field flared upon their seeing. Boats iridescent and angular hastened toward the harboring comforts of land. By guile or skill or favorable chance their pilots had outraced the pulsing afternoon's sterner insurrections.

As for that other race, Steven's formidable contest with Ryan, what the two of them had agreed would be a realistic calculation of their seamanship and of the boats whose speed they'd be commanding—as for that race, Ryan had claimed a solid victory. For that reason she and Steven anticipated that this shrewd interpreter of the sky's signs and portents and of a fleet rival's surprised eclipse would regard the race as his and with canny foresight navigate his vessel homeward. There he would revel amiably and not with the preening self-regard that uses victory to deny the skills of an enterprising comrade. Instead Ryan would, they believed, recognize an opponent's merit. More than that, he would salute the bond between athletic peers which had drawn into their fraternity two proficient young ladies who brought to a nautical adventure their own extemporaneous daring.

While they hastened across the subtle billow of waters that seemed as sensitive to the flicker of a pushing wind as to the aureate-blueness of an ambiguous sky, Steven would, from time to time, look back at the flash of catboats and cutters not far behind him. He expected to find Ryan and Tracy rising assured and splendid with their sailboat, there in the loom and sweep of onrushing nearness—right there, on the curve and slope and crescent slant of the sea. But only the wind rose then, its gathered powers held tense and indeterminate within a throbbing nature.

Later, a half-hour or so, while their sailboat skimmed across the wheeling bay, they at the rudder discovered new the zinc-white hang of wind-bleached cliffs glaring like the sea-tossed bones of a devoured world. Right after that with startled awareness they looked back at the rugged sky and ragged clouds and uneasy surge of waters thrown into the pivoting hurl of receding distance. Then, reassured and believing, they saw splendid Ryan and exhilarant Tracy hurrying windward toward them while scaling sea-whelmed altitudes of risk—all its gravity and mass and supple fervencies.

How comforting in that moment to witness out of their hope and expectation the elated presence of Ryan and Tracy riding on the cantering sea. But all too soon gusts of prismatic light and rippled outlines and surfaces subverted as mirage or illusion what they were seeing. Before their eyes Ryan and Tracy disappeared. Not without a tinge of wistful humor, she and Steven understood with pensive dismay that they had been seeing what was not there. They had been devising rather than finding the solacing imagery which in too-excited apprehension they beheld.

As they arrived home and the wind, bestirred, was pushing them into the shadow-flecked dock, they lowered their storm sail and with quicksilver motion rolled and lashed it to the boom, around which they had looped the mainsheet so that with one pull on the end it could, as if gliding, unravel. Adept and precise, Steven now guided the tiller in and turned broadside to the dock just before reaching it. Then old grizzled Quinn hobbled along the pier to meet the heave of Steven's mooring line and, afterwards, struggle onto the boat to help them cover the boom with tarpaulin. They tied it snugly over the furled sail and at the sides below the gunwales, with both ends left open to keep air moving through. They meant to store the vessel in the boathouse, away from the heft and hurl of the summer storm.

Once more they looked back to the dark, rougher waters that were roiled again and voyaging alone. By this time whole squadrons of catboats and cutters and yawls had hurried back to other jetties and piers and private docks near or within Brenton Point. Some of them had hurried forward to charted destinations or unexpected harbors away from home—and beyond the horizon of violet-grays and reds and orange-yellows that to their searching eyes flickered like temporary flame or a vaguely perceptible beacon. As they looked back, they paused on the rim of uneasy apprehension to confirm what their eyes and reason and intuition had already taught them. Ryan and Tracy would not in that hour be returning. Nor would they return in any of the other hours which with jagged and weighty powers were still to influence that wayward afternoon.

Massive burnt-umber clouds, cumulous and sky-welling and with the wind proprietary over the sea, were heralding further inroads of storm. Why Ryan had chosen to outrace this eddying risk, she and Steven could not—except prodded as they were by the doubtful accuracy of surmise—begin to fathom. Perhaps, Ryan had consented so intensively to the race on the sea, that he had no need to justify safe hesitation or the prudent retreat that promises security even while subverting the adventurous purposes inspiriting a young man's bold nature.

Or possibly the very turbulence of the impending storm had quickened his determination to race not against

Steven, but against wind and wave and sky. Or a calculated desire to wage battle with chance and accident had eclipsed his otherwise shrewd appraisal of things—his realistic awareness of options and probabilities. Or, just as likely, he expected the storm to be as brief as it was wild and, thus, unable to prevent his returning with Tracy in a few hours.

Whatever the truth of things that would in time echo clearly, they had no misgivings about Ryan's ability to deliver Tracy and himself to the sanctuary of a convenient shore or distant island. He was an accomplished adventurer on the sea. His tested skill and hardened agility were a far more convincing surety than too-cautious aptitude or dutiful mediocrity.

No, she—like Steven—had not one misgiving about Ryan's confident proficiencies or about the resourceful equipoise which he had always maintained between his aggressive sailing and the sea's arbitrary fluctuations.

Rather, it was the thought of Tracy that gave her pause. Her sister's venturousness was a complicated imagery that perplexed even while it appealed to her solicitude for her. That Tracy's casual repudiation of safe convention—this rebellious hour soaring alone with Ryan across a storm-rankled bay—could do her much harm, she was uneasily aware. Though, in league with Ryan, she might well elude the sea's fiercer convolutions, her sister could, because of carefree behavior perceived as reckless and sensual, compromise her good name.

That they, each of them singular and attentive and witnessing the world as if new in their seeing, were expected to represent established traditions and rigorous standards and the subtle codes which were the language of their rank and prerogative, Linda's matter-of-fact understanding of their social group's ruling constraints and judgments wisely acknowledged. In that summer of 1920, the men and women who were the leaders of the privileged society to which they belonged observed the four of them and appraised, as though they might prove valued possessions, the resilience and integrity of their characters. They noted subtleties of gesture and spirited assurance and searched out all the hidden correspondences between intimating outlines and colorful surfaces and that startling emphasis individuality. All the while they imposed upon the estimated imagery that was apparently themselves, four young beings evolving, permissible definitions that carried with them the vested interpretations of an entire class.

So she understood, pensive in her uneasiness about Tracy and Ryan riding together over ominous waters. But only for a moment would she allow these thoughts to give her pause.

Perhaps it was at this time that she felt the full weight of her unease, with its complicated structures of quiet disdain for society's narrowness and troubling surprise at Ryan's casual regard of Tracy's safety and of her reputation. She had turned with Steven away from the dock and had noticed in the lift and flare of her hurrying glance whole shafts of raveling sunlight pierce a brooding mass of ocher and gray-blue clouds. A moment after that, Quinn called out to Steven the question that prodded the pulse of his discomfort. With three young workmen, the aged mariner was preparing to carry the yawl from shoreline waters to the boathouse nearby. It was exactly then that she felt the full weight of her unease.

(So she explained to Olivia hours later, recounting to her that wayward day while the Coast Guard kept searching for Tracy and Ryan.)

What she so clearly recollected were the raspy timbres of Quinn's gravel-rough voice and the grizzled features of that hard, wily man meeting directly Steven's own inquiring frown. His young, furrowed brow had been a way to evoke once more from a tough old sailor the simple words that had been overtaken by the rippling wind's taut fluctuations.

"Will Mr. Turner and the young lady be coming back today?"

It was Steven's turn now, upon hearing the echo of Quinn's question, to repeat himself by once more looking back at the sinuous disarrangement of indigo waters, which were sun-flashing still, yet restless. To her eyes, they were almost aggressive.

"I don't know" was all he cared to answer.

Then, with well-honed watchfulness and while pausing with her on the path to his parents' summer home, he scanned once again the storm-imminent waters. Their ambiance of gold and purple still rode over umber traces while he searched for other signs of Ryan and Tracy sailing homeward across the roused velocities of that nearly completed afternoon. But only the wind hurried forward, a welling of currents like wilder symmetries. Hurrying, too, were the leaning verticalities of hills and trees on the southwest rim of the bay. Nearer than that and more emphatic, a sudden trio of sloops, gray-white and wave-tossed, headed for other harbors. Still the tang and fumes and fish-scent of the sea teased the senses. Suddenly a roiling of sun-rippled clouds and lightning ignited raw tension upon the billowing land.

Turning now from this flare of chance and ominous energy, this flash and surge and italic notice of the day's hazardous aptitudes, she and Steven met the silver-stone path that brought them to the north wing of the house. Unobtrusively they found their way inside a private entrance and the seclusion of his father's study. Once there, amidst the solace of pastel walls, they were all the while conscious of newer clarities and crispness and the cool harmonies of opaque blue. They knew again the plush of a Beauvais carpet, ample chairs and desk of cherry wood, and gilt-edged bookshelves with special editions. On the periphery of their seeing, outdoors with the storm-glimmering afternoon and brushing against the beveled window they sequestered, swaying profusions of golden leaves and red-winged fruit belonged to an aureum maple.

In the heightened awareness of all these sensuous things, she stood before an illuminating portrait of Steven's parents. As if she had come to this room for that very purpose, she studied their quiet strength and the quiet felicities of their union. Then, she turned to Steven, who was already speaking to someone from his father's personal house-phone. He was telling Chapman, the indispensable overseer of this large and demanding Newport home, that it was necessary for the senior Mr. Bradford and Mr. Maguire to confer with him in the study.

3

"You've done all that can be done," Steven's father asserted, without suggesting that his son's swiftness in alerting the Coast Guard about Ryan and Tracy's being caught somewhere over storm-lashed waters would necessarily resolve their peril or any of the other unexpected dispositions of the last hour or two.

Nor would her father allow himself even the hint of a frown, to his disciplined mind a prosaic sign of dismay, that Steven had, by consenting to a reckless venturing with the sea, too casually relaxed his guardian care of others and of himself. She sensed that he recognized none the less the mute anxiety that Steven was holding at bay because of his self-command and his keen-eyed intelligence.

Without attracting to themselves any gratuitous inquiry, the two men had drawn away from the festive summering ongoing still, though no longer in the surge and sway of wind-roused greenery or on the splendid flower-redolent terrace. The guests, she learned, had hurried from the storm into spacious rooms that married Tudor stateliness to the Bradfords' witty evocation of a pastoralism offering the simplicity of its natural powers to an artful elegance. This sumptuous July happiness, this tincture of illusion belonging to their privileged class, seemed therefore never completely separated from the earthbound gravity of the real. In due time Daniel Bradford and her father had withdrawn from that magnificent array of rooms where the exuberant voices and self-reflexive conversations of the guests accepted the more mellifluous intonations of piano and flute and viola. They accepted as well from outside a surround of French doors the disharmonies of roused winds and roiling thunder.

In curious apprehension they had arrived to notice, there inside the hushed ambiance of Daniel's study, the austerities of Steven's and her responses. Steven's clipped speech and stoic demeanor and tautened physicality would—she was certain—suggest at once that something was wrong.

(She was aware that these senior men knew Steven well—Daniel because he was his father and her own father because he was Steven's godparent. With quiet appreciation, they were acquainted with many of his virtues. They regarded him as an admirable war hero. Right after law school, Steven had fought with hardened fury at Cambrai and Messines and afterwards at St. Mihiel. At the last, he'd fought in the Meuse-Argonne offensive, where the enemy's bullet pierced his body at a point only an inch or so from his heart. Until that moment, he had heard all around him the rapid, incessant guns and fired alongside his platoon his own stuttering rifle's accurate bullets. Bitter experience it was to see his closest comrades die like cattle, sometimes in the cool of a sunlit morning when their muscular bodies, meeting the enemy's volleys, lifted and broke apart.

Time and circumstance had tested Steven and found him to be strong-willed and brave. During these few years succeeding the war, he had found his way back to a promising life. Only recently, scrupulous directors had in pleased unanimity invited him to a junior partnership with the international association of lawyers in which the Bradfords—Daniel and his brother—and the Tomlinsons—his wife's father and uncle—shared with British and French colleagues the primary influences.)

When these older men had in heightened awareness arrived at Daniel's study, they noticed not only the stoic demeanor of her reliable Steven. They noticed as well within her face an unanticipated stillness and a careful reserve.

Arriving there to meet their tense decorum— Steven's and hers—and meeting it, to apprehend the uncertainty of the moment, Daniel and her father allowed themselves to gather each of them within the protective folds of their embrace. Perhaps so lighthearted a greeting might dispel the nearly imperceptible pall that glanced at their equanimity. In spite of their unease, they were braving out whatever adversity had already called them to itself.

"Come," Daniel said, while with modulated authority guiding them now to the masculine solidity of comfortable Empire chairs. The indigo-gray tints of glimmering light, a scanning motion as of the wind perceived upon the beveled window nearby, offered other comforts. "Tell us what, on such a remarkable day, has brought you to, of all places, my study."

Influenced at once by this diplomatic expression of his father's solicitude, Steven quickly recounted all that had happened in the past hour or two. He compassed his way with unflinching directness because only then could he with integrity proceed to explain.

He described to the two men the exhilaration with which he and the others had acceded to the late afternoon's promise of adventure. Forthright, he spoke of the impulse which had pushed him into so rash an enterprise—his banked capacities for a wilder courage suddenly and without warning ignited. He explained all of it, reliable man that he was and very much his own individual. Then he waited coolly, standing with her in composed alliance, while her father summoned the words that would hurry them forward to the things that they must do and not do. Her father was once again assertive Liam Maguire, roused in this moment from the lethargy that grief had imposed upon him.

"We must not tell the other guests," he said, addressing himself to Daniel as well as to Steven and her. The even timbres of his voice (a taut fluency now) as much as his silver hair and bronzed patrician features granted him a cultivated man's authenticity. "There is nothing they can do to help, at least not at the moment. And their too freely speaking of the matter might, without their intending it, only make the situation appear more grievous than it really is."

Her father further declared that they must proceed with the evening as though nothing untoward had happened. In an hour or so they must join the society of guests—twelve from that afternoon's prestigious gathering—who as weekend visitors would be the privileged recipients of Olivia Bradford's superb candle-lit dinner. With exemplary tact, he chose reasonable words meant to influence their better judgment. While doing so, he selected a supplementary language of gesture—a cultivated wave of his hand at the perimeter of brusqueness and a rugged and impatient shuffling of his Spartan frame. With the insight of a steadfast friend, he wanted to suggest that not even the wayward episode involving Tracy and Ryan should permit Daniel or Steven and her to alter the rules that required them to maintain, as much as they could, the durable harmonies of the evening.

With the proficient modulations of a man for whom behaving well must always be an active principle, he reminded her as well as Daniel and Steven of their more pressing obligations. He intended to assure the Bradfords that their return to the evening's original promises would help their cause immensely, hers and her father's, by deflecting attention from this temporary mischance involving her sister and Ryan Turner.

"I believe no harm has come to Tracy or to Ryan," he said, having urged them to go forward to the evening's festive offerings. "They are waiting out the storm somewhere, safe in a convenient place."

In any other context, she knew, her father would have regarded as intemperate so emphatic an optimism before the stern laws of risk and accident. But there in Daniel's well-appointed study, all of them held now in unresolved tension, he found optimism a worthy ally for his purposes. He meant to dispel their unease and put them in mind of the implicated blessings of earlier hours.

"This has been such a lovely day," he declared with a supreme effort of will. "I refuse to believe it will bring harm to any of us."

Tough-minded and resilient, her father was suggesting a way for them to proceed. With self-willed assurance, they must represent their useful capacities for standing with perfect equipoise before uncertainty.

Confronting this ambivalent episode involving his younger daughter and Malcolm Turner's son, her father was once more his assertive and leaderly self. All through these summer weeks, he had expressed with taciturn dignity the lonely offices of prolonged grief, imparted as they were by his inveterate discipline and by the rigorous philosophy that held anguish in, oblique and private. From time to time he had secluded himself with Tracy and with her. He was adjusting slowly to his wife's having died six months earlier and to this vacant afterward which was unmitigated by those flickering moments when he believed her to be so inexpressibly in the sun-touched shadows of the room with him and their daughters.

In this moment, he appeared to have left his grief behind him. The news of the boating misadventure had—she could see—roused the same spirit that had made him a formidable leader of Maguire industries as diverse as lumber and textiles, oil, copper and diamonds, and real estate.

"We must do everything that we can to make this evening a first-rate experience," he said. "And we must not neglect our round of golf tomorrow afternoon."

He directed these last words to Daniel and Steven.

Daniel admired her father's spirit and wanted to accommodate his brave optimism. Drawn into the shifting complexities of the hour, he intended to defer to her father's austere self-command. Steven, who with an assertive glance had already signaled his own will, also agreed that they must bring a lighthearted presence to the evening unfolding around them.

After all, a festive dinner offered as an ornament of a summer night, even a storm-laden one, requires the presence of a host and most—if not all—of his guests. Were the host to be absent, he would excite if not inquiry, the stillness of apprehension. So, accepting the good sense of her father's plan and understanding that the Coast Guard would keep them informed about the search for Ryan and Tracy, Daniel and Steven turned to the serener requirements of the evening.

As soon as he could (while he was dressing for dinner, she learned afterward), Daniel told his wife without explaining any of it that Tracy and Ryan would not be joining the dinner party. There would be time, he knew, to explain all of it later, without in that moment casting a pall upon his wife's exuberance. For in alliance with their meticulous staff she had prepared a proper celebration for their guests. He understood, of course, that even in the full knowledge of the afternoon's wayward surprise, she would have guided the evening to felicitous purposes. Olivia was, after all, a cultivated woman with sufficient experience of the world to respond sensibly to its bruising liabilities.

When she was once more alone with her father in the suite of rooms that the Bradfords had offered them during these weeks of their visit, Linda voiced her concern. She spoke quietly, not wanting her father to detect the enmity for Ryan that had risen in her ever since the hour of the boat race.

"What Ryan has done is wrong," she said. She was adjusting his bow tie just before they would make their way to the Bradfords' party. "He should be punished. His being with Tracy in this way compromises her good name."

"You mustn't worry about this matter," her father said, patting her shoulder affectionately. "Everything will turn out the way it should."

His words appeased her anticipation of the punishment that awaited Ryan. Yet she would not relinquish her look of sisterly concern. She did, however, offer her father a gentle kiss. She wanted him to know that his words pleased her.

He was going to say more. But the wind, furious and untrammeled, hurled its weight against the house as if to remind those listening that it had not yet finished with them. In mid-sentence, her father paused. Only then was she aware of how skillfully he had been disguising the more visible nuances of his apprehension. Sternly mastering whatever alarm could overtake him, he hurried forward on the momentum of new words.

"Malcolm Turner's son knows how to protect himself and protect others," he said, with a grudging respect of the young man about whom he was speaking. "Don't you worry about him or about your sister."

"But I am worried," she said. "I'm worried for her reputation. This little adventure will cost her far more than it costs Ryan."

"When all is said and done, she'll not be hurt by what's happened today," he said. "I promise you that."

Again she felt nearly solaced by this suggestion that Ryan would be duly punished because of his careless use of the day and of her sister. In the same instant, she heard music floating from the dining room and, while she and her father hurried to that festive scene, she imagined the scenarios that would call Ryan to account for his wayward conduct.

That Malcolm Turner would be involved in this meting out to his son a proper punishment, she felt certain. Just before he began dressing for dinner, her father had telephoned Ryan's father. What words they had exchanged, she did not know, because her father had closed his bedroom door before he began the conversation. She knew that the punishment would not involve scandalizing the Turner name by bringing Ryan to a court that might send him to prison. That punishment would bring scandal to Tracy, as well. Instead, she imagined, Ryan might be compelled to enter military service or to accept an indefinite exile to Europe. Whatever happened, her father would do everything to protect Tracy's name.

It was Tracy's happiness which was, before all else, the most important issue. Ever since she had come into the world, he had accorded this daughter a special, though unobtrusive, advocacy, because she needed from him a show of affectionate support far more than she herself had at any time during her girlhood. Tracy needed as well his careful attention and a willingness on his part to sympathize with her disappointments. Aware of her need, he had cultivated a loving and teacherly counsel that received with respectful demeanor her idiosyncratic aptitudes and that embraced always even her smallest achievements.

Year after year his fatherly acumen had harnessed his approval of Tracy's efforts to a sensible decorum. At the same time, he had maintained a care not to offer her any affection which would overshadow his love for her, his first-born daughter. His was a judicious mindfulness of the obligations which every right-thinking father gladly fulfills toward each of his daughters. But he imparted toward Tracy, nonetheless, a tactful solicitude and a firmly balanced protectiveness. This intuitive collaboration with her emotional needs might, he believed, compensate for her mother's refusal to coddle or favor in any manner this second of their daughters. Although she had confessed to thinking so only once, her mother regarded Tracy as a difficult and overly sensitive girl. She wanted her to become strong-willed and self-reliant, as her older daughter was and as she herself had, long ago, learned to become. Not for her was the spiritless femininity that clings inordinately to masculine prerogative.

Whether it was this insistence that her daughters cultivate a wise assurance which influenced her muted impatience with Tracy or her association of Tracy with the grievous losses which her fate compelled her to endure, her mother never told her. So mysterious sometimes was the heart that pulsed within this soft-spoken woman whom her father had chosen as his life's companion. But when she was a self-assured girl of fifteen, her father did tell her of this problem involving her mother's relationship with Tracy. On that afternoon, during her summer recess from school, her father had called her into his study to suggest that she devote a portion of her vacation to her eight-year-old sister. For some time now he had noticed how subtly his wife distanced herself from Tracy. Because her coldness toward the child dismayed him, he occasionally reminded her of the girl's extraordinary capacities. In these conversations, he urged her, an admirable woman flawless in all respects except this, toward a finer encouragement of their younger daughter's affirming self-regard.

Her mother's subdued enmity toward Tracy had begun, he felt, on the very day that Tracy was born. For her birth made a hard delivery that had nearly cost her mother her life and thereafter impaired her once-beaming constitution. Yet only three years later, while dismissing the protests of her physicians and after with rigorous disciplines nurturing a semblance of her once-prevailing strength, she consented to carry a third child. For much of her pregnancy she accepted the imprisoning bed-rest and fastidious nursing which her doctors prescribed to ensure a safe delivery. But, despite her cautious regimen, the infant was still-born. Its death compelled within her heart new waves of bitterness, because she had lost the son for whom she and her Liam had prayed.

It was this same bitterness which, her father reluctantly admitted, had at that time hovered about his own unease. It arrived before him as if to watch the workings of his soul made visible. At that time he, too, avoided as much as he could any contact with her sister. He had consigned her, an ingratiating three-year-old, to the care of her quietly efficient governess. For this last of her pregnancies had sealed his wife's fate. Or so the most eminent of her cardiologists told her. With cautious attention to her health, she might live another decade or even two. But no longer could she, with her husband, travel as much through the world as had been their wont, nor could they socialize as often.

Not for long, though, did her father carry a secret bitterness in his heart. Only after a few weeks of his withdrawal from Tracy did he hurry to embrace her and, ever after, albeit with a more restrained approval, offer her a proper father's encouragement. As far as his busy schedule in those days allowed, he tried to compensate for the loneliness and uncertainty her mother's carefully modulated reserve wrought upon her.

She was not surprised that he forgave Tracy the first transgression to which she had willed herself. Nor was she surprised that he would impose upon Ryan a suitable penalty for misusing the younger of his daughters, whose innocent heart—he told himself—beat so tenderly. For her father, the only wonder was that Tracy had declared her independence so openly. But, though there had been a show of courage in her consent to share Ryan's romantic adventure, she had journeyed into the unknown too soon. Of her hesitation about the way she should navigate her individuality beyond these fugitive hours, the immediate aftermath of her adventure would leave no doubt.

As astute as he was compassionate in his responses toward her, her father would concede that, by means of her elopement with daring young Ryan, whom she was convinced she loved profoundly, his troubled second daughter had made a tremendous leap forward to the personal autonomy she had not yet successfully negotiated. In time, with his fatherly guidance and the guidance of other caring teachers, Tracy would become strong enough to stand alone without his support and—as the Fates must allow—without Ryan. But for now, because he would see to it that Ryan hurried on to his own young destiny and because she was not yet ready to stand by herself, wholly sufficient, Tracy needed to stand with him. Quietly acknowledging that need, he would guide her toward a life far more fulfilling than the inordinate excitement which Ryan was offering her on this storm-roused day.

This, she told herself, was her father's point of view. Believing so, she consented with a poised conviviality to the Bradfords' glamorous dinner party. In the midst of loyal friends and newfound acquaintances, she felt supremely contented. She was even more pleased when

Olivia Bradford whispered to her some favorable news. The full powers of the storm, its occasional rebellions notwithstanding, had merely glanced at their shores. Even more favorable, the Coast Guard, with whom Daniel and her father had been communicating all that evening, had found no evidence of any craft coming to harm. She and her father, as well as the Bradfords, were of course relieved, though still uneasy not knowing just where Ryan and Tracy might be.

A few hours later, after all the other guests had retired to their rooms in the main house or to the guest cottages nearby, she and her father sat conversing with the Bradfords within the burnished amenities of the parlor. There, each of them sipped a cordial or wine or black tea from India, while they touched upon subjects as varied as Mozart, the Summer Olympics, the latest Bentley, and Wall Street. Later, they would admit with lighthearted banter that, though they liked each other's company immensely, they had delayed retiring to their rooms because they wanted to be instantly available to receive any further news about Tracy and Ryan.

When their vigil had lasted forty-five minutes, the call from the Coast Guard came, telling them that Ryan and Tracy were safe in Bristol. They had taken shelter at an inn before the hurl of the storm could harm them.

Only then did she with her father and Steven with his parents agree that they should get some rest. The oncoming day promised to be a very busy one.

As they were making their way to their rooms, Steven turned to her father. Like them, he was very pleased to hear that Ryan and Tracy were safe.

"This problem with Ryan and Tracy is working itself out, after all," he declared with sturdy confidence.

To this remark her father, first to enter the hallway, without looking back at him offered a casual-seeming response that banked the energies of its analytic temperament. As if to consent to Steven's forecast and at the same time express a reservation, elliptical though it might be, about the idea that any problem by its own devices could work itself out, he held in check the full heft of a wise realism. Instead, her father allowed for the contingencies that sometimes shape a deed or consequence and even initiate occasionally an auspicious direction for our lives.

"Well, if it isn't going to be all right," he said, "we can try to make it so."

4

How far from being all right everything was, to their startlement and dismay they learned the next morning. Two young Coast Guard officers, Jeremy Britten and Erik Douglas, from boyhood days fishing pals of Steven and since early summer venture-rousing friends of Ryan, had accelerated rather than merely accompanied Ryan's and Tracy's prompt and discreet return from Bristol. In a private conference the summary of which she learned from Olivia afterward, they quietly informed her father and Malcolm Turner, who had an hour earlier arrived from his summer home in Nantucket, about the wayward episode into which Ryan had entangled Tracy as well as himself.

They began by speaking of Ryan with that ingrained respect and admiration which capable men accord prowess and aggressiveness. With a flash of recognition that the potency of Ryan's young daring was not unlike their own wild comfort with adventurous chance, they praised his expertise, coolly rendered, in outracing the storm. They also mentioned favorably his clearheaded success in bringing Tracy to the sheltering amenities of Bristol Inn. More than once they remarked upon the courtesy and equanimity that never failed him, not even when confronted by the angry scene that had erupted at the inn early that morning.

But they said all these things as a preface (shrewdly calculated, her father bethought himself later) to all the other words that needed saying. Duty-bound to stringent regulations, they had to report to Tracy's father and to Ryan's, too, that Ryan Turner, riding on the cusp of a storm-bruised day, had brought himself and Tracy dangerously near the path of a scandal.

"Without meaning to, he's got himself and the young lady into a bit of a tangle," Jeremy explained.

His magisterial height and hard blue eyes transformed wind-burned physicality into someone commanding. As he met directly the probing inquiry of the two men before him, he was all the while measuring the weight of precisely chosen words upon the taut self-containment of her dignified father and upon the subdued concern, as genuine though without the tautness, of Daniel.

"But he's a first-rate fellow all the same," Erik interposed, quickly speaking on Ryan's behalf.

The older men noticed, and were to mention later, his ruddy confidence and that of his cohort. They noticed, too, how lightly cynicism influenced their dutiful attentiveness. Tough-minded, they could gather still the plausible words meant to exonerate their friend's questionable intentions.

What had happened at the inn at eight o'clock that morning, as though the unexpected episode, as swift as it was rancorous, were coiling intricacies of malice about Tracy and Ryan, nearly compromised the Maguires' good name. Having outraced the hurl of the storm on the sea, these two rebellious individuals had in the roiling flare of the preceding afternoon presented themselves at the inn as a newly-married couple.

In that hour the assailing wind was rising against the white clapboard eaves of the large colonial house (carefully restored and retaining still its original imagery as a sea-captain's property). The pulsive rain thrashed across sky-blown waves of summer-fragrant trees, a profusion of symmetries all plum and peach and almond flowering italic and sovereign over the wide expanse of emerald greenery. Wondrously in wind and rain did that wind-sown splendor glide and ascend and scale storm-crossed altitudes. At the same time the frantic rain lashed the graveled path hurrying away from fertile woodlands behind the house. Not only the rain but the sweep and whirl and swell of wind kept battering the inn's columns and eaves, gables and windows and sloping roof-top. Cobalt-blue wicker chairs were toppling across a velvet-soft lawn before croquet hoops and mallet and ball. Conservative guests, roused in the lift and surge and liability of a momentary reprieve from hum-drum routine, hastened with their children to indoor comforts.

Perhaps it was the rush and swerve and startlement of so kinetic a scene that lent a plausibility to Ryan and Tracy's being in their unanticipated arrival all that they said they were— young marrieds from the Bradford estate eluding a stormy bay's rising powers. Or possibly it was the chance happening that Mr. and Mrs. Collins, keepers of the inn, were so held to the worry of the storm and intent upon battening down the large house and grounds from late afternoon's incoming betrayals that they, as well as their staff and guests, could at first offer scant attention to Ryan and Tracy's arrival. There was a naturalness, shaping its own spontaneity, to their being suddenly there and they also hastening to escape the storm's brute treacheries. It was that, perhaps, which made them plausible. Or, more likely, Ryan's affability and directness quickly won the Collinses' approval and Tracy's demureness pleased.

Whether it was all of these things or only some of them or one more than any other that influenced the innkeeper and his wife, as well as their staff and guests, to accept Ryan and Tracy as wholly authentic, neither she nor her father ever learned. Nor did Tracy tell when she described to her and their father the specific unfolding of that fateful day.

What words first described their time at the inn, Ryan and Tracy's, were an elliptical translation of all that had happened there glancing at the harsh truth through subtlety and indirection. Those words belonged to the two Coast Guardsmen, Erik and Jeremy, who meant with calculated understatement to justify their venture-rousing friend and his warm-hearted young lady. As tersely as they could and as impassively, they informed her father and Daniel that Ryan and Tracy, pretending to be married, had brought an angry scene upon themselves, as well as the ugly threat of being detained or arrested.

That the two Coast Guardsmen were willing to reveal this much, and more, of what others were calling the young couple's subversion of public morality reflected the diplomatic compromise they had made with the sheriff of Bristol. As if they were crafty strategists negotiating in the spirit of truce or détente or apparent reparation, they were gaining far more for Ryan and Tracy than they had permitted themselves to forfeit. What they were forfeiting, though only to her father and to Daniel, was their silence about the episode. Leagued momentarily with the innkeepers, they had by pledging away that silence held at bay the unexpected adversary who had threatened to expose Tracy and Ryan to public disgrace.

In this subtle partnership with the Coast Guardsmen, it was the keepers of the inn, Bartley and Maureen Collins, who were essential to the swift efforts they had all made to protect the young couple from so stern and precipitate an adversary as Warren Thompson. Within the first hours of seeing them, the Collinses decided they liked the "idea" of Ryan and Tracy, who were so romantic and life-loving. As they themselves had once done, these two extraordinary people were making their way without the consent of their parents. (When Ryan explained his and Tracy's situation to them, he took care to mention all those concerned with a calm and respectful deference.)

What a lift to the spirit it was, even in that first fleet witness after they had been called away momentarily from the business of securing the imperiled house from the rising storm, to come approve the two strangers hurrying still out of the distance toward the beleaguered inn. The Collinses had been alerted to the surprise of them by their goodhearted secretary and sometime clerk Mrs. Reed, who had kept watch at the desk while others worked to protect the house from the storm. Watching, she saw from the southeast corner the two of them hastening with agile fluency along the wind-torn road that stretched away from the harbor and met, coiling and accurate, the graveled path that would guide them to the waiting colonial inn.

By that time the Collinses were standing within the burnished stability of the reception area ready to greet them and, greeting, scan their healthy glow before returning to the task of safeguarding the house from the weather. It was wonderful and mysterious and italic to see them so suddenly there and passing on their way to them with supple ease through the white glistening portico sinuous about the house, its columns and pillars hand-hewn and "southernized". Their brightness passed as well along the spacious entry hall by limestone hearth and Shaker child's chair and cauldrons of brass filled with cedar-scented firewood.

Confidently arriving, they paused beneath rafters pendulous with antique baskets and pomegranate medallion quilts and sprigs of orange-hued bittersweet. Then, their bearings quietly affirmed, they continued on to the polished-oak reception desk. Luminous behind it against the wall, a brocaded green tapestry carried as its Gaelic salutation an invocation and spirited wish and affecting beneficence: *Caed Mille Failte*—one hundred thousand welcomes.

Afterward, resourceful Ryan and amenable Tracy refreshed themselves, secluded and liberal in the comforting pleasures of their room. Then, bathed and contented, they came to the affable society of the candle-lit parlor to share with other guests their experience of art and music, sport and adventure and travel. Always they melded their language to enthusiasm as fluent and vital as the occasions in which, stirred by the press of desire or venturous aptitude or activity memorable and enhancing, they had consummated its privileges. Later, too, when they enjoyed a festive meal within the colorful traceries of the dining room, they were in those public hours responsive to the others there with them in random alliance happily met at the splendid table where, mutual and expansive, they found themselves together.

That evening, of the thirty-two guests residing at the spacious inn, seven or eight enjoying dinner with them were inspired (so the Collinses later told Olivia Bradford) by Ryan's and Tracy's heartening anecdotes. Ryan told them of his hunting red stag in Patagonia. He also spoke of tracking the elusive whitetail buck in the pinyan-juniper forests of Montana and of cycling through the Chang Tang region of the Tibetan Plateau in China. Tracy recounted her visits to France and to British Columbia. She also spoke of skiing in Vermont and of flying with her father in a Curtiss PW-8. In turn the other guests also shared narratives about their own explorations scanning the kinetic surprise that was one's self extemporaneous in the world, negotiating possibility. They, all of them there together, were a most compatible society. If not proven confederates, they were potential allies recognizing in each other correspondent energies.

What a lift it was, the Collinses were to agree, as they summarized to Olivia afterward the complete surprise of that day. What a spark it was, igniting their own memories of early passion that surged beyond the ordinary measures of joy, to notice the love in Ryan Turner's eyes as he cast his heated glance upon Tracy. From time to time and with decorous modesty, she met that glance, so that everyone there observing them at the table believed them to be an ideal married couple. While moving about the tables to supervise their staff's care of the guests, Mr. and Mrs. Collins observed them as well. They found themselves especially pleased that chance had brought to their inn, as though they were a gift or godsend for a stormy evening, these two vibrant persons who had influenced a few wearying and ominous hours to become one of life's happier occasions.

5

Ryan and Tracy had planned all of it together, this game of pretending to be married which would draw them into an adventure of their own making. With restless anticipation, her sister consented to whatever devices she with Ryan might impose upon its wayward subtexts. That, in these several weeks of being guests of the Bradfords, they had come in secret to know each other well was all to the good—the good, that is, of their liberated purposes. They were enclosed, though, within a group of their peers.

From time to time they were aware as well of Steven and her dutifully watching from a distance while allowing all of them, seven or eight, a provisional freedom. Carefully observed, Ryan and Tracy could claim a promising intimacy only by availing themselves of the enshadowed path or unobtrusive alcove or sequestering arbor.

At first they had to pretend that they were attracted primarily to their team of friends and not to each other particularly. Whenever casual occasions or summer celebrations called them to join the group, they behaved toward one another as nothing more than courteous allies. Yet with Ryan even obliquely, Tracy regarded their proximity as an extraordinary hour. Theirs was a nearness that suggested. It became a subtler emphasis receiving togetherness as a union of themselves alone even when attended by well-bred girls and hardy youths and personable chaperones.

It was thrilling to be with each other even obliquely, while, with their exuberant friends and dutiful chaperones still there as an affable necessity, they swam in the Bradfords' cantilevered pool where the blue-green waters flowed as if by magic into the Atlantic. On other inspiriting days they went cantering along the soft turf of that portion of the Bradfords' estate given over to a capacious horse farm. There, while riding a tawny-colored Welsh Cob or an Austrian Haflinger with chestnut body and flaxen mane, they sometimes jumped fences. Their hands and arms stretched forward to follow the movement of the horse's head and neck. Adept riders, each of them remained perfectly still and correctly balanced over the horse, thereby leaving the horse free to jump athletically over the fence. On other days they sailed over Newport waters, found themselves exuberant at a county fair, and—as a foursome who included Steven and her—rode in a De Havilland D.H.50 which Steven and Ryan co-piloted.

Then there came those times when they were alone. They would most often meet within a thatched-roof summer cottage which stood a half-mile from the Bradfords' home, yet on their property none the less. With its gable detailing, the cottage recalled the pavilion spread of a Japanese house. Far more spacious than a conventional cottage, this guesthouse enjoyed a sheltered location. All around it were full-grown evergreens, a Momi fir, red cedars, mugho pines, and Japanese hollies. White-tinged Japanese painted fern highlighted a shaded corner outside the cottage.

Here, because the house was currently unoccupied, Ryan made love to Tracy.

Twice, he made love to her within a wisteria-covered gazebo which a small bridge linked to a pond. The delicate whiteness of Iris ensata played against the dark waters of the rock-lined pond.

He was devising the episode by which, in a setting more secure than a gazebo or a cottage where a gardener or groundskeeper might interrupt their lovemaking, they could consummate their love without any chance of being discovered. Being of his class, she meant far more to him than the occasional girls who had from time to time satisfied his sexual needs. He wanted to protect her from the harm of gossip or from the penalties invoked by a narrow community. For him, Tracy was an altogether different experience. The two of them were, he told himself, in mind and spirit already married.

So it was through this idea—a convincing assertion of their bond with each other—that he came to persuade her of the rightness of his plan. At a picturesque inn within the secluded seaport of Bristol, they would—in fragrant privacies and without the Church's approving seal or any other legal document permitting them—celebrate once more the marriage of their bodies to one another. At first they would register as the husband and wife their own personal laws made them. That they, by so appearing, would attain a comfortable marriage room for the union of their souls and bodies, even as they subverted narrow convention and protected Tracy from the public's accusing eyes, would serve well to enhance their mutual pleasure.

"How clever you are," Tracy said just before kissing him once more, exhilarated and breathless.

"There are many ways to have an adventure," he told her. His full, sensual lips caressed now the exquisite lobe of her right ear. "We'll wait awhile and find the proper day for this one to begin."

They had to wait merely a week. For the Bradfords' grand summer party provided the ideal occasion for launching their rebellious flight. Ryan's challenging Steven to a boat race over restless waters initiated an adequate scenario. It became a lighthearted enterprise for stealing away from familial watchfulness. But the storm interfered with the swift unfolding of his plan to elude temporarily the Bradfords and Liam Maguire and, at a solacing inn, to enjoy a few blissful hours with this loving girl for whom his passion had amply grown. They'd imagined that they would return, sated and inspirited, to explain that they had merely been sailing the exciting race that he and Steven had agreed to wager. Even when the storm rose to mar his plan to go back to the Bradfords by early evening, Ryan did not waver.

Although he rightly calculated, with his cynical awareness of the world, that the randomness of things might gainsay his efforts, he permitted himself to imagine that he and Tracy could, once they had smoothly arrived at Bristol Inn, telephone the Bradfords to declare that all was well and that the inn was happily providing them attractive shelter within the propriety of separate rooms. (They would be wearing the gold wedding bands he'd won in a poker game while he was vacationing in Buenos Aires. He had won them from an exiled Frenchman, a corrupt banker trafficking now in the black market.)

But, the storm assailing Bristol's telephone lines, Ryan could not make the call that would mollify the startled authority they had left behind them. Nor could he return with Tracy on the evening of that day. Both the

Coast Guard and local police were to come in search of them, complicating his deftly constructed scenario. Yet, in spite of them all, he and Tracy still achieved their love, enjoying in a secluded room at the inn a union of their bodies and spirit and wilder nature.

So Tracy was to tell her, referring to her experience of those hours as the best happiness of her life thus far.

6

But early the following day a rancorous scene dispelled whatever solace the evening had granted them. For Warren Thompson, the sheriff of the town, had come to the inn searching for a young man and an even younger girl who, when caught on the storm-roused waters of Narragansett Bay, might have by luck or quick wit or a lithe acumen found their way to land and to adequate shelter. Having, during the previous afternoon's rising turbulence, been alerted by the Coast Guard about the missing pair, Sheriff Thompson—at some peril to himself— had been scouting about the houses nearest to the water, until toppled tree-limbs in the middle of primary roads and street-floods from the lashing rains deterred his search. Then in the morning, after the storm had ended and safe passages, because of the work of vigorous crews, were beginning to be restored, he (still searching) had come to the Collinses' inn. There, he discovered that Ryan and

Tracy had registered as a married couple and had spent the night together.

Sheriff Thompson was a gaunt, stern man of forty. The bronze of his skin was a summer emphasis for so personal a reality as his gray-black crew cut and cold, brown eyes, as well as his aquiline nose and tight-lipped self-command. His tall, rangy frame rose to an extraordinary six-foot, four inches and enhanced his military bearing. There were within him subtly visible traces of rigorous judgments and lacerating disciplines, of unflinching severity and a brooding cynicism. In spite of his hardened demeanor, the Collinses liked him. Bartley and Maureen had capacities for glimpsing, a little at least, into the bruised soul or fragmented spirit or battered heart. Their affection was also inspired by his being true to the Spartan code that, they felt, must have helped him make sense of things.

His parents had been loyal friends of Mrs. Collins' aunt and had, before she died, spent many afternoons or evenings visiting with her at the inn and even at times helping her in the very busy summer season. As if fostering their own variant of this friendship, Warren and his wife had stayed at the inn during the first few anniversaries of their marriage. They were favorably disposed toward the kind and long-widowed woman and toward the equally hardworking Collinses. How happy Warren and Louise were in those days. (So the Collinses from time to time later recalled.) The young sheriff and his wife were conscious, while savoring present joys, of the bright promises their tomorrows held for them.

Afterward, they were happiest when they had their first child, a healthy boy. By the time he was nine years old, this son called forth an earlier imagery of his father's cool, level gaze and his supple physicality. Already, he had acquired an affinity for the tests of courage and stamina his father was wont to devise on his behalf, the better to shape properly his masculine powers. Some of those powers the boy was discovering through soldierly marching formations and calisthenics and swimming. Habits like precision drills became ingrained, addictive mastery.

But then everything changed. The boy, Warren's namesake and in subtle ways something of his alter ego, a second self growing into a parallel identity, died of pneumonia right after his eleventh birthday. The child had taken ill when his father, heedless of Louise's cautious petitioning not to go, brought the boy to his first experience of hunting rabbits inside the autumn rawness of the Bristol woods. After the boy died, flushed with fever and, to the last, fighting the strange, breathtaking malady, the two of them—Warren and Louise—were never to each other the same. Whatever brightness they together had once achieved had, with the boy, burnt out its light.

Bitter and grief-struck and guilty, Warren could not locate within himself a strategy that would help his Louise to see how lost he was. Instead, with tough-skinned taciturnity and longer hours at his work as the sheriff of

Bristol, he salvaged the exterior part of himself that had not been destroyed. But he had no art or will to find the words that could guide her into his soul. There were between them no intimate conversations that would help her to recall how elated the boy had always been to hone, with his father's coaching, early aptitudes for fishing and boxing, soccer and swimming and gymnastics. Each of them had been a test and validation of his emerging prowess and a promise that he, too, would one day be as tall and sturdy and knowing as his father.

Without being offered any of those words as his way to call out his grief to her, she began to regard him as a stranger, arbitrary and inhuman. All his familiar masculine responses that had seemed protective now appeared to her new eyes as an insidious method of controlling not only the boy's life, but her own as well. Again and again he had deferred to his will alone. Her will had been an ancillary volition meant to be, in relation to him, merely feminine and assenting.

Eventually, he saw in her accusing sullenness flashes of contempt and hatred and a dark refusal to forgive him, even were he—months after the boy's dying— to find the necessary, penitent phrases. So they turned away from each other, except for the few times, raging with desire and loneliness and despair, he took her by force. On those nights, Warren Thompson experienced through his mastering potency the fiercer ecstasy that comes to those men whose confident bodies are roused with keener appetite in the very act of dominating frail and resisting loveliness.

Yet, in spite of her disdain and her fear of his primitive fury, she found her hatred falling away from her. From time to time and only by chance now, she met his haunted gaze upon her. It was a gaze as well of tender love and of mute yearning. His intelligent brow was usually caught in a frown. Now the full lips whose pressing touch upon her own had once brought her immense pleasure curved downward in a grimace, a sign she read as his raw and wounding self-hatred.

Because she felt that he could no longer in any of the essential ways solace her, she left him five months after their son had died. She returned at first to her parents' home in Dover, Delaware, and eventually, after the divorce which through his lawyer he protested, she found her way back to a less complicated happiness. By then she had met again, while in a wholly new way perceiving, a gentle fellow from her high school days who had become a dedicated veterinarian and lived a solitary bachelor's existence. He'd never moved past the emotional alliance which they had in an earlier, platonic season made.

It was after they'd married that Warren Thompson, bereft and angry, understood clearly, as though it were a prophecy his own actions had delivered, all his happiness was now behind him.

On that sun-tinted July morning two years later when, at the Collins' inn, he confronted Ryan and Tracy,

Warren Thompson was indeed a bitter man. The sight of them together at breakfast, rapt in each other as if transported still by desire wakened and fulfilled, roused in him a despairing envy of their happiness. That same ease and contentment, he and Louise had once enjoyed. In the beginning, the love they'd experienced together had become their own symmetry. With him, she'd consented to a carnality that was for body and mind and spirit a solacing excitement. The painful truth that at the last he'd taken by force the soft pleasures of her body he believed by law were his to possess made him despair of his fate all over again in the instant he observed Ryan and Tracy. Quite apart from his envy of their happiness and his grief over his personal loss—and yet inciting his anger just as keenly—was the goading thought that, from a privileged class, they believed they were their own law, above restrictive codes and admonishing conventions.

Whether it was that thought more even than his quiet despair that influenced Warren's hostility toward Ryan and Tracy, Mrs. Collins would not allow herself to guess. She remembered only the brooding manner in which, at the threshold of the crowded dining room, he watched while her husband, without inviting the concern of any other guest, made his way to them. In cordial harmony with the requirements of the moment, she stood beside Sheriff Thompson as he sighted lovely Tracy with venturous Ryan. By this time her husband had quietly approached them.

They were a most romantic couple, seated as they were by a spacious window that overlooked the tranquil, iridescent bay. Sailboats in the distance and swimmers not far from shore were already navigating the luminous waters. Mrs. Collins observed how the sight of them brought to Warren's tension a face whose chiseled profile suggested, almost imperceptibly, the intricacies of anguish. As if it were a casual gesture, she drew him, while slipping her hand gently through the curve of his rugged arm, away from the threshold to the privacy of Bartley's office. She did not want any guests to connect his pausing there on the rim of the room—to search out, perhaps, before going urgently forward—to the young couple whom she and her husband regarded still as ideal, whether they were married or single.

"You've broken the law," Sheriff Thompson said, confronting Ryan and Tracy with accusation stark and threatening the moment they'd entered Bartley's office. "You've lied about being married and have had carnal relations with each other."

Ryan comforted at once a startled Tracy with a gallant pressure of his hand upon her own. He positioned himself in front of her and thereby protected her from this unexpected adversary. Then he moved forward to face Warren Thompson with unflinching directness.

"We've done no wrong," he asserted coolly, "and, as for being married, we are—in soul and spirit and body. We need no legal paper to tell us so."

"That's not the way we think around here," Warren said. "But it's a good way to get yourselves arrested."

"Whatever has happened between us concerns ourselves and nobody else."

It was then that the Collinses, Bartley and Maureen, noticed Warren's hand drawing from his windbreaker a metallic jangle of handcuffs. Quickly they stepped between the sheriff and this youth they had grown to admire.

"Let it alone, Warren," Bartley said, the rich timbres of his Irish inflections respectful, yet counseling a friend nonetheless. "Let it be. These are fine young people."

The sheriff, without looking at him, for his sullen eyes were all the while fixed in appraisal of Ryan, resisted the burly innkeeper's words.

"You're out of line, Bart," he said. "There's been a violation of the law here."

"These are fine young people," the strong-minded innkeeper declared once more. His echoing thought was another way for Warren to see.

"They've brought harm to no one," Maureen added.

The crisp fluency of her voice drew Warren's attention now to her calm and fetching demeanor.

"If you carry this further than it need be carried, you will bring harm to us and to our inn"

Perhaps it was their addressing him in the name of the long friendship they'd shared with him that tempered the harshness of Sheriff Thompson's judgment.

Or perhaps it was the happy chance that, at this moment precisely, wise Mrs. Reed appeared. Her silver hair and brown, gentle eyes; her delicate nose; and her mouth and chin granted her large, motherly girth a benevolent dignity. She was ushering into the room the two Coast Guardsmen, Jeremy Britten and Erik Douglas. Several hours earlier, they'd located Ryan's boat in the harbor. After verifying that Ryan Turner and Tracy Maguire were safely housed at the inn, they had telephoned the Bradfords that all was well. Then, without disturbing their friend Ryan and his young lady, they'd told Bartley that they would, out of deference to Mr. Maguire and Mr. Bradford accompany Ryan and Tracy home.

But first they must respond to an urgent call from their commanding officer directing them, just then, to assist an elderly widow. That good woman was stranded in her flooded cottage on a graveled road the wind-driven rains had nearly washed away. She needed safe passage to the inn, where the Collinses would prepare a room for her. So, having now returned, delivering the grateful widow to the reception desk, the two Coast Guardsmen proceeded to join Bartley and Maureen. Subtly, they shaped a plan for the young couple that would, in the sheriff's eyes, bring them to the equivalent of a stern tribunal or a judicious hearing.

Perhaps it was the Coast Guardsmen's timely arrival which influenced the sheriff most of all. And possibly it was, a little at least, Warren Thompson's ambivalent regard of the two young romantics that tempered his hard will. He had a grudging respect for Ryan's manly directness and a pulsing awareness of Tracy's extraordinary beauty and her refinement. He noticed how quietly she had recovered her poise while mooring it to its own, natural demureness. She and Ryan expressed a passionate love not so very unlike the one that he and Louise had in their best years known together.

Whatever truth hid itself within these possibilities, the Collinses, upon retiring to their rooms that evening and even in later reminiscence with Olivia, could not with certainty declare to each other. They simply acknowledged that the plan they had quietly devised, in league with the quick-wittedness of the Coast Guardsmen, may have been the catalyst which saved Ryan and Tracy from a scandal. For Warren, whose rigid principles needed to be satisfied, agreed—though with some reluctance—that Erik and Jeremy would accompany Miss Maguire and Mr. Turner back to the home of their hosts, the upright Bradfords. There, they would duly inform her father and Malcolm Turner of what the sheriff deemed to be the young couple's wrongdoing. Having heard only good things of Mr. Maguire and of Mr. Turner, he was reasonably convinced that, as solid citizens, they would bring upon Ryan and Tracy a proper punishment.

7

"You've had an exciting weekend," Malcolm Turner asserted with casual ambivalence.

He was closely observing this bright arrogance before him—- this complicated Ryan who was his only heir. The cool light of the room revealed that Malcolm's muscular physique was finely honed and, at forty-six, impressive still. That morning she scanned his rugged features and found in them the nearly imperceptible scar buried across the left side of his face. It was a fading emblem of the grievous war wound he had sustained in battle on the sea against turbulent Spain at the close of the nineteenth century. The radiance of that same light noticed his curly gray hair and thick, dapper mustache. His was a diplomatic emphasis of individuality that still maintained its own laws and privileges.

"But you have forgotten your obligations to the name you carry and to the well-being of this young lady."

They were standing directly before him now, his prepossessing son with her fair-skinned sister. Two in so italic an alliance might have, had the circumstance been apt and permissible, represented to her quiet observation an extraordinary romantic ideal. They were standing as if poised and united before him in the Bradfords' main parlor and within the resourceful witness of her father and of Daniel Bradford, as well as of Steven and her. These reliable fathers had agreed to see the wayward couple minutes after exchanging cordial, parting words with the quick-witted Coast Guardsmen. During this meeting with the Coast Guardsmen, she and Steven had brought Tracy and Ryan, dazzling still even while waiting on the rim of uncertainty, to the east wing of the house—apart from any chance encounter with the affable guests with whom Olivia would later that day be leaving for an afternoon's excursion to Newport's summer-festival atmosphere.

Only after that meeting did they accompany Tracy and Ryan to the parlor. At this time, Daniel, Steven and she remained as anchoring influences over Malcolm and her father, as well as over Tracy and Ryan. They had come with modulated aptitudes to mediate, if need be, the tenser liabilities of this meeting.

"We had an afternoon's adventure, sir," Ryan explained while keenly measuring the weight of his words upon the three older men.

From comments that he had made to her and to Steven in the weeks just passed, he had made it clear that he respected these men. He respected their self-command and their achievements. With his pragmatic calculations for measuring the heft of a person's character, he perceived them as authentic. Their quests drew them always to the wider world—to its perilous enterprises and its manifold rewards. It was in that turbulent and uncertain world, in territories not unlike those over which his father and the other men prevailed, where he intended to activate whatever larger capacities waited to be summoned from within himself.

She imagined that he understood these men well. His was a youth's unobtrusive empathy which recognized in them his own advocacy of brave and rigorous explorations. Because of that, he held himself in clipped and pertinent understatement while standing with Tracy before them. Nor did he betray his conviction that he and Tracy, expressing freely in a summery room so natural an ardor as their passion for each other, had done no wrong.

"We found the inn while the storm was becoming dangerous," he said, his matter-of-factness mooring itself to a temperate assurance. "But no harm has come to either of us."

Her father, disappointed in this casual-seeming viewpoint, quickly demurred.

"What happened at the inn, your being in that room together as a married couple, is a dark blame upon your character," he said. "You've compromised Tracy's honor and your own as well."

"Oh, Father, you don't know how it is with us," her sister hurried to explain. Her voice was matter-of-fact and assertive. "Ryan and I are in love and will be in love for the rest of our lives."

She paused before the thought that would help them to see even more clearly the way it was between Ryan and her.

"I don't believe that my being at the inn with Ryan was wrong," she said. "But if you gentlemen think it was, then we're willing to face the consequences."

With understated solidarity, the three older men glanced at each other. Her sister's words had obviously pleased them.

"In that case," Malcolm said, "our meeting should go very well."

He was speaking for her father and for Daniel and Steven, as well as for himself. No sooner had he made his remark, than the four of them accompanied Tracy and Ryan into Daniel's study.

At this time, she excused herself because (she imagined) Steven and her father would not want her to be involved any further in a scene which was already fraught with many tensions. That this private conference—with its legal underpinnings—would involve not only the two fathers, but also Daniel and Steven as judicious mediators once more roused her expectation that both Ryan and her sister were going to be punished. They had broken the rules and needed to be punished.

For the next hour, she assisted Olivia's able gardeners in the careful transfer of camellias from the conservatory to a southerly corner of the garden nearest the main house. There, for the rest of the summer, the camellias would thrive within an alliance of full sun and dappled, occasional shade.

When she had completed that task, she found herself especially pleased that she had brought both a poised calm and a rational purpose to what might have loomed as an uneasy time of waiting. Only then did she permit herself to return to the main house and to the parlor that stood as if observing the closed door to Daniel's study.

In the first few minutes that she sat waiting, she could hear excited voices emanating from the study. No sooner was her curiosity roused in a new way, than Chapman came into the parlor. Bowing as he passed her, he hurried on to the study to deliver the tray of champagne which Daniel had apparently requested.

She rose from her chair slowly, because she was trying to fit together the fragments of the puzzling scenario unfolding before her. In that very instant, right after opening the door of the study to receive Chapman with the tray of wine, Olivia Bradford—noticing her—hurried forward.

Daniel had called his wife to the room twenty minutes earlier. He as well as those four others with whom he had been conferring in his study wanted to share their news with her. Malcolm had already telephoned the good news to his wife, who had stayed behind in Nantucket to orchestrate a convivial day with six of their New York friends. So Olivia explained, as she invited her to join what promised to be a moment all of them would remember.

"It has all been arranged, my dear," she said. "Ryan and Tracy will be married in two weeks."

Only by remaining very still could she find her way to what she hoped was an acceptable response.

"I can't believe that my father would agree to such a marriage," she said. "Tracy isn't ready to take that step. Nor is Ryan."

"But your father and Malcolm won't have it any other way," Olivia said. "They want them to be married. They've wanted it for a long time."

"My father never mentioned it to me."

"He never mentioned it to anyone else apparently, except Malcolm," Olivia said. "From time to time, the two of them have had serious discussions about the possibility of uniting the Maguires and the Turners through Tracy and Ryan. Their weekend adventure convinced your father and Malcolm that the time was just right for a marriage between the two."

"It isn't right," she protested. "They're being rewarded for having done wrong."

"Is it so wrong to fall in love?" Olivia asked. "You should see how happy Tracy and Ryan are. Everything has worked in their favor."

Linda frowned, unable to conceal her angry dismay.

Noticing her unease, Olivia patted her shoulder gently before offering her some motherly counsel.

"Be happy for your sister," she said. "Be happy that she is happy. Her dream has come true, and that is a very rare thing, indeed."

"I want her to be happy," she assured her. "But I'm still very worried. Ryan may not be the man who can bring her a lasting happiness."

"She thinks he will," Olivia said. "She's ready to take a leap into the unknown, and that is all that really matters."

"Perhaps you are right," she agreed diplomatically. "I'll hope for her sake that you are."

"Of course I am right," Olivia declared while smiling. She sounded brisk and lighthearted. "I know when two people are very much in love. I have only to look at Ryan and Tracy together, and I know."

They were moving now toward the study where—she saw in the distance—Malcolm, Daniel, Steven and her father were already raising their glasses to the young couple who would soon be married.

She would join them in their conviviality. She would smile and even laugh and, if there were songs to be sung, she would sing. She would embrace her sister and embrace Ryan, too. She was prepared to accept him, because to do otherwise would betray her bitter memory of his playing with her affection. For a few weeks, while she and Steven were in his company, he had quietly seduced her with the intensity of his casual gaze and the smoothness of his words. Then, when she had begun to give him her heart, he had turned away from her the instant he met her sister.

Toward him, she too would be casual and as friendly as the rules allowed. But never would she forgive him for having played so carelessly with her desire.

ABOUT THE AUTHOR

David Orsini is a Phi Beta Kappa graduate of Brown University. He has taught literature and composition in secondary schools and colleges within Rhode Island. In addition to *The Subtleties of Seduction*, his books include *The Weaver of Plots*; *The Woman Who Loved Too Well*; *The Ghost Lovers*; *Vanishing by Degrees*; *Bitterness / Seven Stories*; and *Schemes, Disguises, & Traps.*

Visit www.quaternitybooks.com.